Freshly arrived fr
Lizzie Banister, a
Gray has laid ey
adventurer, he ha
new land of Austra
opals and true love
Lizzie continue to
amorous advances with have nothing further to do
with him when she is faced with the choice of the
workhouse or his protection?

By the same author in Masquerade:

MY LADY IMPOSTOR

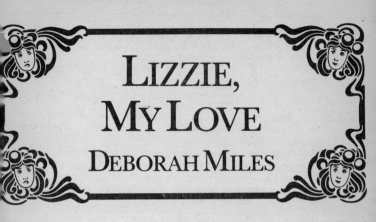

LIZZIE, MY LOVE

DEBORAH MILES

MILLS & BOON LIMITED
London · Sydney · Toronto

First published in Great Britain 1984
by Mills & Boon Limited, 15–16 Brook's Mews,
London W1A 1DR

ISBN 0 263 74619 4

Set in 11 on 11 pt Linotron Times
04/0484

Photoset by Rowland Phototypesetting Ltd
Bury St Edmunds, Suffolk
Made and printed in Great Britain by
Cox & Wyman Ltd, Reading

CHAPTER
ONE

LIZZIE paused by the bulwark, leaning against the thick salt-scented wood, and gazing rapt at the grey, rolling sea. Big brown eyes dreamed on days past and days to come. 'I want to see the world, I want to go places!' had been her heart's cry ever since she turned ten and had seen how grim and hopeless her adult future seemed, stretched out before her like a bleak, sooty tunnel.

'You'll go and stir the soup, and then you'll tend to your baby sister,' had been her mother's answer. Her mother was dead by the time Lizzie reached fifteen, her baby sister in a home for the homeless. Lizzie had already been in service in a big, impersonal London town house. She had found a sort of pride in shining silver and polishing Chippendale. She had found pride, too, in the cook teaching her to read and speak 'proper', and learning a little of the world outside great, grubby London. 'I reckon as you could be a lady's maid, if you were to work at it,' the cook told her, the most glowing tribute Cook could pay anyone. But it was not to be.

The deck was swarming with life. Seamen climbed the riggings, swabbed decks and toiled with ropes. The passengers strolled or sat, chatting and laughing and sitting silently, lost in contemplation, like Lizzie, of the past and future. The *Governor* was not a new ship. She had been on the Australian run for some years past, ever since she

was adjudged too old and slow for trade to the
Indies. She was an ugly ship, but somehow comfortable with it.

Someone tapped Lizzie's arm, and she turned
with a start. A plump, but petite girl with flushed
cheeks, aged about seventeen plomped down beside her. 'Blimey, it's hot!'

Big blue eyes, their guilelessness belying a glint
of cunning, surveyed the other passengers and
alighted on the nearest available male, the middle-
aged, unsympathetic doctor. Jane fluttered her
lashes at him, and he bowed at her, flushing under
his luxurious side-whiskers.

'Jane! Must you behave like a . . . a hoyden?'

Lizzie had been looking after her sister Jane ever
since her mother had told her to, but of late Jane
had become more and more troublesome. She
laughed now, tossing her blonde mane. The two
sisters were bounty girls, in this year of 1834, which
meant that when they were landed at Sydney
Town, the owner of the *Governor* would be paid a
certain amount for each girl. It was no wonder most
bounty ships were packed to capacity and more.
Women were still a rarity in the new colony, the
men far outnumbering them. Women were there-
fore being encouraged to emigrate, and advertise-
ments blazoned on London streets how good life
was in Australia. The workhouses and orphanages
were flooded with leaflets, listing the wonders of
the new colony. Employers, said the print, were
begging women to work for them, and the women
were naming their own price! Husbands were
swarming like flies—rich and poor alike. It was the
land of opportunity, a virtual paradise, and Lizzie
had been drawn by the glowing accounts like an
alley cat to a saucer of country cream.

'Name our own price!' she had cried to Jane, when the two girls met on Sunday afternoon, the only day they were free to do so. Jane's blue eyes sparkled like sunlight on water.

'Husbands! God Almighty, Lizzie, it sounds like heaven on earth.'

'Don't be vulgar, and don't be blasphemous,' Lizzie retorted, but more from habit than any belief that she could change her sister's ways. Besides, her thoughts were far too busy with planning and scheming: if they could pool their money they might have enough for the necessities of shipboard life, and as it was a bounty ship they would have their passage paid for them. And if they got work immediately on arrival, they would be well up on their outlay!

They had nothing to lose, that was for sure. Lizzie had toiled constantly during most of her twenty-five years. There had been no wealthy parents to shelter her from the degradation of poverty, and Lizzie had laundered and stitched when still a toddler, to help her mother feed the fatherless family. When she was five, she had been farmed out to a factory, and when she was ten had been lucky enough to go into service. She remained there until she was twenty-four, and ill-health had caused her employers to place her in the workhouse. For the past year she had remained there, firstly recovering from the almost fatal fever she had contracted, and then working at cleaning and stitching in the house itself.

Jane, who had gone into an orphanage when their mother died, had had a more chequered career. She had been shunted around from house to house as a youngster, until at twelve she was put into service. The endless drudgery of routine and

pride in work had bored her, just as it had suited
her sister's orderly mind. She ran away, at sixteen,
and had a spell in the House of Correction before
being returned to duty.

'You'll be the death of me, you will!' Lizzie had
cried, when she came to see her sister.

Jane had wept repentantly and promised never
to stray from the path again. But the temptations in
London were endless, and Lizzie could see her
sister was not strong enough to resist them. Australia would be good for Jane. She could find steady
work there, where no one would know about her
past record. She could start again; they both could.

Only things had not gone as smoothly as Lizzie
had planned, once they were aboard the old *Governor*. As well as being a bounty ship, the *Governor*
carried paying passengers, up in the saloon quarters. The girls had the midships to themselves; a
big, sprawling, open living quarters in which they
slept, and lived, and ate. The mariners had the
steerage for their quarters, but the more luxurious
saloon was for the twenty wealthy passengers
travelling in comfort to Sydney Town on business
or pleasure.

Jane was a pretty girl, and the attention she had
been subject to since they sailed went to her head.
Lizzie had learned to frown at the seamen who
were always hanging about, hoping for a smile or a
chat. They were easily quelled. It was the saloon
passengers with whom she had difficulty. When
Jane appeared in her shabby bonnet, they came
down from the saloon deck to tease and flirt like
dapper magpies attracted by the plumage of a
parrot. And one could not simply frown at a gentleman passing the time of day, nor could she threaten
him with informing the captain, as she did the

common seamen. In fact there was nothing she could do but stick close to her sister in the self-appointed position of chaperon, and be as unwelcoming as possible. Most of them seemed to get the message eventually.

'You encourage them!' Lizzie hissed, when Jane had been particularly outrageous.

Jane tossed her head, her pretty face flushed with triumph. 'It's so boring, Lizzie, and I like them. Why shouldn't we talk? They're gentlemen, aren't they? Not any old rubbish? You're always saying as how real gentlemen are worth a dozen . . .'

'Yes, yes, but . . . Jane, you know very well what I mean!'

'We're only talking, Lizzie,' Jane said, and fixed her sister with a mocking blue gaze. 'What are you frightened of?'

Lizzie bit her lip. She had heard well enough from a few of the girls about some of the bounty ships. Lax morals had ended in girls becoming with child on the voyage out, and tales of rapine and virtual orgies caused Lizzie's rather innocent mind to boggle.

But it would never do to tell Jane of them! So she folded her lips and sniffed. 'Never you mind. Just don't encourage them, that's all.'

Jane pulled a face, eyeing her sister with amusement. In some ways she often felt twice as old as Lizzie. Lizzie was such an innocent. 'You're just jealous,' she retorted.

Was she? Lizzie searched her heart for such an emotion, but could find no clear-cut answers. She had looked after Jane for so long it was difficult to allow her to grow up. And yet she was such a child still, in so many ways. Sometimes, when her sister had been particularly vexatious, she would wish she had sailed alone. And then, in the creaking, washing darkness of night, with Jane breathing softly beside her in the crowded midships, she would look at her and see their mother in her and be overcome with love. Jane would always need looking after, and who was there to do it but Lizzie?

'Penny for them?' Jane broke in on her reverie, an elbow jerking into her ribs.

'Ow! I was thinking of home, if you must know.'

'What's at home to think about?' Jane muttered scornfully, and eyed the seaman nearest them, returning his grin with a bashful flutter of black lashes. 'Only a few more weeks to go, so they say,' Jane went on. 'I'll be glad to have my feet on firm land again. How about you, Liz?'

'I won't be sorry.'

'Mr Gray says he can find me work, if you'll let him. You're so frosty to him, Lizzie. He knows you dislike him.'

Mr Gray! That was all she'd heard, ever since the man had come aboard at Cape Town. Mr Gray had caused her nothing but trouble. He had set his sights on Jane from the moment he saw her, and unlike the others, Lizzie could neither quell him nor pretend to herself that he meant nothing by it. She had seen his sort before, while working in the London house. Why, one so-called 'gentleman' had even tried to kiss Lizzie in the passageway! She would never forget the feel of his lips wet on her cheek, and the sudden, dark thrill when his hand fumbled at the starched frill on her bodice. That knowledge still made her blush, even now, and feel ashamed that she could have, for one moment, enjoyed the experience. No, whatever Mr Gray might profess to be, and despite the fact he was travelling first-class, his intentions towards Jane were certainly not honourable!

She had watched her sister and Mr Gray constantly now for some weeks. She had watched the way he teased Jane, sometimes with a mockery only thinly covered with syrup, and sometimes with a look in his eyes which made Lizzie's heart quake unpleasantly. He was dangerous, and single-minded, and wicked. Jane was fascinated. She had never met anyone remotely like him, and thought him the most marvellous thing since the steam train. She tried to return his barbed compliments and innuendos, and did her best to show him how worldly she was. Lizzie feared, however, she was very much out of her league when it came to Mr Gray.

'You're just jealous,' Jane cried, after a particularly virulent outburst. 'Because he likes me and not you! Because he thinks I'm pretty and you're ugly!'

Lizzie had flounced away, deeply hurt by the exchange. Later, she had crept back to their bunk and peered into Jane's little slab of polished glass and taken a long look at herself. Jane was right. She *was* ugly. She had white skin, dead white like a corpse, and her neck was grubby though she tried so hard to put into practice the cleanly habits she had learned in service. And her hair! Wildly curling and black as pitch, it framed her face like a chimney-boy's brush. Brown eyes, the colour of strong tea. Nose too long, and mouth too wide. It was an uncompromising, stubborn face. She scowled, tears brimming in the brown eyes. No, not pretty at all. But—and she dried her tears determinedly—she was honest, and strong, and she could work hard. That must make up for the rest.

Later, Jane had apologised and hugged her. 'I'm sorry, Liz. Really I am. But Mr Gray doesn't mean anything. And even if he did . . . I can handle him. I know I can.' Lizzie had sighed, and forgiven her. But she remembered she was ugly, and the misery of it simmered still beneath the gruff manner she affected to hide her own dangerous vulnerability.

'Mr Gray's coming,' hissed Jane, startling Lizzie with another dig from her elbow.

Lizzie looked up and saw two men. As she looked one of them began to make his way down to their deck. A man of above medium height, quite strongly built. Black hair, a little too long at the collar, and dark eyes, much darker than her own. Skin tanned golden by time spent in a sun much hotter than that of England. Mr Gray had informed the Banister sisters the first time they met that his living was made in Australia, and the sojourn in Cape Town had been for business purposes only.

The other man was following. Taller and slimmer than Gray, he was smoothing his moustache, which he wore with the air of one wearing precious diamonds. His hair was more red than brown, and his eyes a twinkling, kindly grey. Lizzie preferred Mr Jason Wilson to his companion, and made no bones about showing it.

Jane was smoothing her skirts, and biting her lips to make them red. Lizzie caught her eye impatiently. 'I don't know why you bother to make such a fuss,' she said stiffly. 'The man's not worth it.'

'Lizzie!' Jane hissed. 'He knows you don't like him, but you could be polite.'

'I don't care if he does know. I find him totally repugnant.'

'What sort of word is that,' Jane retorted. 'You learned to talk lah-de-dah at that house you were at, but it doesn't mean anything to me.' She glanced up, and her anger faded, her blue eyes suddenly dreamy. 'He's so handsome,' she sighed.

'And knows it!' Lizzie retorted tartly, not usually one to be influenced by outer appearances.

Jane giggled. 'Mr Wilson is more of a coxcomb than Mr Gray.'

'Yes, but . . . there's no harm in him, Jane.' Her plea went unheard.

Jane stepped forward to greet the two men with her prettiest smile. 'Morning, Mr Gray, Mr Wilson. A fine day, is it not?'

Her carefully enunciated words made Lizzie squirm. Mr Gray looked her up and down with obvious pleasure, and something more, a gleam in his eyes that made Lizzie long to box his ears. It was a look of ownership; as though Jane already wore a chain and a collar, diamond-studded of course, and was broken to his hand.

Jane took his smile at face value, and strutted a little, glancing at him coyly under her long, curling lashes. She was a very pretty girl, and had learned to like admiration since they boarded the *Governor*. But Lizzie blushed for her now. Had she no pride at all to look at a man in such an inviting manner?

'A very fine day, now that you're here, Jane,' Mr Gray replied, and his smile was wicked. 'However, I could wish we were off this poxy vessel, and somewhere less . . . crowded.'

'It's not poxy!' Lizzie retorted, missing the by-play, and then wished she'd stayed a scornful observer when they all turned to her. 'It's . . . it's homey,' she went on gruffly, and glared.

Mr Gray raised his eyebrow, and Jane giggled. 'Oh Lizzie, how can you talk so? It's a dreadful old boat!'

The dark eyes shifted from one sister to the other, and their expression of idle indulgence changed to bored politeness. For a moment Lizzie was betrayed into meeting them, something she did as little as possible. Her opinion of him must have been quite plain, because he raised his eyebrows at her, and the silence stretched until she looked away, her pale cheeks flushing a bright pink.

'I find it very difficult to believe you both sisters,' that cool voice said, softly but with a sting. 'You're like . . . honey and vinegar.'

Lizzie clenched her fingers on the stiff cloth of her skirt. 'Jane takes after our mother,' she said coldly.

'Ah, that would be it then!'

His black eyes mocked her with the knowledge that she was the vinegar, while her own shone pure hatred.

'I hardly remember her,' Jane was saying, blithely unaware. 'Liz has been sister and mother to me for a long time now,' she added. 'Lizzie is always so . . . so thorough about things.' She squeezed her sister's arm affectionately, and Lizzie recognised with misgiving the mood that usually preceded Jane doing something particularly outrageous.

Perhaps Gray recognised it too, for he winked at Jane and said aside to his friend, 'Wilson, perhaps you would chat with Miss Banister here, while Jane and I take a stroll. You two always have so much to say to each other.'

Jason Wilson smiled uncertainly, worry marring his brow. 'But, Zek, did not Miss McFarlane ask you to attend her this morning?'

Hezekiah Gray laughed softly, and something in the sound caused the hairs on the back of Lizzie's neck to prickle. Jane giggled, enjoying it all immensely.

'Miss McFarlane wants me to wed and bed her, in that order. Unfortunately, I'm not an orderly man.'

'Gray, I say!' Jason Wilson glanced at Lizzie, apology in his grey eyes, as he straightened his coat. 'There are ladies present, man!'

'Are there?' Gray glanced at Lizzie, his smile mock-apologetic. 'My pardon, Miss Banister.' Jane giggled, as they turned away.

'Miss Banister, allow me to apologise for my friend's behaviour,' Jason Wilson said softly, and Lizzie met the worried grey eyes with stiff features. 'He is unconventional, I know. But it's just his way. He means no offence.'

'No?'

Jason cleared his throat. 'He's the sort of man who cares little what others think, Miss Banister. Perhaps that's a good thing. I sometimes think we worry too much about how we look to our friends and associates, and worry too little about our own happiness.'

Lizzie sniffed.

A pause. 'Miss Banister,' and he sounded suddenly urgent. 'Zek Gray is my friend, but I feel I must warn you. Miss Banister, you seem to me a most intelligent woman, and that is more than I could say, I beg pardon, for your pretty sister.'

Lizzie was all attention now, though all she said was, 'Jane is very young.'

'Zek enjoys the company of women, and makes no bones about it. Your sister shouldn't construe too much from his . . . partiality towards her.'

'If you mean to tell me he's not about to call the banns, I know that well enough!'

'Miss Banister,' he said, more urgent than before, 'if it were merely a flirtation I would not speak, and if I thought your pretty sister was . . . well, wise to the game, so to speak, I would not speak. But I think she is young, and flattered, and I see that you worry for her and seek to protect her. I speak as much for your sake as hers. My friend is a man who takes what he wants, Miss Banister. It would not occur to him that his actions were in any way reprehensible—your sister has been as eager in her pursuit as he in his, Miss Banister.'

Lizzie frowned. 'You mean to tell me he would ruin my sister, and leave her to face the consequences?'

Jason Wilson opened his mouth and closed it again. He bowed his head with a sigh.

'And he means to do this to my sister?'

'I feel sure, before we make landfall, he means to . . . well . . .'

Lizzie knew what he meant. And she knew, too, that Jane was silly enough and infatuated enough to offer little or no resistance. And then she would be ruined, and by such a one as Hezekiah Gray. It must not be.

'Miss Banister?'

She had forgotten Jason Wilson, and looked up with the light of battle in her brown eyes. 'Thank you, sir. You've been most generous in informing me of this . . . well, I thank you with all my heart.'

He sighed, relieved of his burden of guilt. He admired this girl, and pitied her. Hezekiah annoyed him often with his careless attitudes to convention, and perhaps he was a little jealous that someone should have so little conscience. It would do him good for once to be outwitted by Miss Elizabeth Banister. 'Thank *you*, Miss Banister,' he said with sincerity.

Lizzie glanced down the deck, watching as Gray and Jane dawdled by the gangway to the steerage. Jane was laughing up into his face, and as she watched Gray stooped and whispered something in her ear, managing to brush her cheek with his lips as he did so. His attitude was suddenly so predatory that Lizzie shivered. He would not have her, he would not! She was determined on it. And when Lizzie was determined on something it usually came to pass.

CHAPTER
TWO

FOR A moment Lizzie lay in the darkness, heart thudding, still caught in the nightmare which had woken her from her slumber. The ship creaked about her, the sound mingling with the snores and sighs of the women lying in the stuffy midships, serving out their long sentence of waiting before reaching their new homeland.

Thinking of it made Lizzie sigh, and she turned over, shivering a little under the thin cover of the blanket. She frowned, and reached out a hand to the space beside her. 'Jane?'

The space was empty.

She sat up, pushing her unruly hair out of her eyes and gazing about her, thinking . . . hoping, her sister may have felt ill and risen to go to the porthole for some air. But the big, stuffy room was full of prone bodies, and no Jane.

A sudden tremor shook her, composed of fear and anger. Jane! No wonder she had been so affectionate this evening, her conscience must have been troubling her mightily. And no wonder she had hugged Lizzie when she tried to make her see sense about Mr Gray and said, 'I can look after myself, you know!' What had they been speaking of? The stars, that was it. Jane had been wide-eyed over how much Zek Gray seemed to know about them. Good God, would she really go up on deck and meet him? She knew the women were not allowed up there after dark!

Without a word, Lizzie began to pull on her boots, and swung her shawl about her head and shoulders, to keep out the worst of the cold. She tiptoed across the planks, and, her mind whirling with those tales of rapine, slipped out of the door into the passageway.

Up on deck she was alone. The sea lay dark and heaving all about them, broken by the darker patterns of the ship's spars and rigging. The only sounds were those of water and ship, interspersed with the man-made sounds of the piano tinkling from the direction of the saloon, and the soft laughter of the seamen from the steerage. Above her, the sky was awash with stars, more than she had ever seen in London, and so clear and close. For a moment she forgot her mission in the wonder of the sky, and stood gazing upwards, the evening breeze tossing the ends of the shawl and moulding her woollen nightgown to her slim body.

'Jane?'

The whisper came from behind her, and she spun around. The man was standing a short distance from her, full in the starlight, while she was in the shadow of the cabin. She would have known him even if it were pitch dark. The arrogant stance, the way he held his head. Words of fury cluttered her tongue, and while she was still trying to sort out some comprehensible sentence, he came forward to stand before her, and wrapped strong arms about her.

Suddenly, she was pressed against a hard, masculine chest, her face smothered by his shirt, his heart beating in her ear, her body a captive of his. The experience was surprising and so novel to her, she was stunned, and stood, letting him hold her.

'Jane?' the voice whispered. 'I thought you weren't coming, you minx. I shouldn't have doubted you, should I? Even your dragon sister couldn't keep you from me, hmm?'

Rage stiffened her, but already his hands had tightened about her, pushing her bosom to his shirt-front. The faint scent of cologne mingled with the odour of tobacco from the smoky saloon. 'You've undressed for the occasion, I see,' he murmured, mocking her, and his lips came down hard on hers.

For a moment she was too surprised to do anything but allow the experience to wash over her, reminding her vaguely of that other stolen kiss. He was kissing her cheeks, her closed eyelids, then her mouth again. Little, light kisses, deepening suddenly with passion, as though the game were over and the serious business had begun. She lay pliant, dizzy and oddly loath to break the spell.

He rested a moment, his cheek to her brow, and she felt his hands warm as he smoothed her back and shoulders. His quick catch of breath brought her out of her reverie, and for a moment she thought he was going to thrust her from him, but then he had relaxed again and was caressing her again. But more urgently now, so that she became afraid and began to struggle to be free.

'Ah no, you'll not escape me so easily,' he hissed, like a stage villain Lizzie had once seen, and squeezed her so hard her breath went. He began to kiss her again, a long, practised kiss designed to force her response. By this time Lizzie was quite dizzy with emotions. She tingled with them, and ached for she knew not what. Her head was pounding, and her breath uneven. She began, unthinkingly, to kiss him back.

'That's better,' he whispered, and she could have sworn he was laughing at her.

She put her arms about his neck, and his hands slid down to the small of her back, pressing her against his own body. She knew then, quite suddenly, that she would never be able to get close enough to him, and the thought shocked her profoundly, so that she was hardly aware of him sliding his warm palm up over her ribs, to cup her breast.

His breathing had grown alarmingly fast, and he whispered against her ear, 'Who would have thought you'd be such a little furnace.' Then, 'I know you want me as much as I want you. I can feel your heart beating for me.' The warm hand squeezed her, making her stiffen with sudden terror.

Lizzie jerked away like one bitten, and stood facing him, her head thrown back, her bosom heaving. 'You lecher! You would have ruined my sister, but you'll not ruin me!'

For a moment the dark figure was still, and then, unbelievably, he laughed. She stared, and started forward as he went on laughing.

'I'm sorry,' he managed after a moment, 'but you sounded so much like a penny romance, I . . .' he took a shaky breath, running his fingers back through his hair. 'Didn't you enjoy my play-acting,' he said in more serious tones. 'As soon as I knew it was you I redoubled my efforts to please.'

'But . . . you mean you knew it was me?'

'Of course. You and your sister are hardly similar in build, are you?' She knew he had raised his eyebrow, even though it was too dark to see properly. 'Why did you substitute for your sister, Miss Banister? Are you sacrificing yourself at the altar of her questionable innocence? Giving yourself up to the big, bad man in her place?'

The light from the saloon windows above fell on his features as he came forward. He was smiling his dangerous smile, and the black eyes gleamed like oil on water. 'Well?' he said. 'I thought you'd faint in my arms, but you enjoyed it, didn't you? Who'd have thought it!'

Lizzie felt her temper rising to ungovernable heights, mixed to an even more explosive brew by humiliation and hurt. She had always had a temper, but managed to keep it in check. Girls with no money and a lot of pride could not afford to have tempers. But now it was soaring to unimagined heights as she faced this loathsome, drawling rake.

'I would as soon kiss a . . . a slug as you,' she gasped. 'You vain, strutting monster. I've seen better men than you in the Clerkenwell gutters.'

She heard his indrawn breath, and knew he was angry. 'Indeed,' he said, his voice like ice. She had never seen Mr Gray angry before, and by the sound of his voice she was glad she could not see him now. Some of her own rage wavered. 'You should be grateful that I gave you the chance to be my paramour, Miss Banister,' he added with cold mockery. 'Let me hasten to assure you I would never have made such an offer in other circumstances.'

'How dare you presume I would wish you to!'

He laughed softly, making her step back although he had not moved. 'Come, come, Miss Banister. You enjoyed it as much as I; have the honesty to admit it. You squirmed over me for more.'

'I did not, you toad!'

He caught her arm, but she pulled away, glaring at him and breathing hard. 'Have I hurt its feelings,' he murmured in soft, steely tones. Then, brusquely, 'Your sister is at least honest about what she wants and doesn't want. You have to hide your feelings under a vinegary exterior!'

'I hate you.'

He laughed. 'So we're down to the basics now, are we?'

'You toad.'

'You've called me that already, Miss Banister.' He hesitated, and when he spoke again his voice was almost a purr, 'I've always liked a bit of vinegar in a woman. Too much sweetness is cloying. Vinegar gives an exciting tartness, an extra challenge.'

'You don't seriously expect me to—'

'To believe I find you attractive? But I do!' he laughed again, and caught her upper arms. 'I do indeed. You hate me, and that's a challenge in itself.'

Something in the way he was standing suddenly shot her through with fear, and she tried to pull herself away and run. He pulled her back even as she moved, and held her against him so hard her breath puffed out of her lungs. She closed her eyes as he stooped to kiss her, only thinking how rough and hurtful he was. He was a callous, cruel lecher, a wicked, black-hearted . . .

'Don't fold your lips like that, girl!' he hissed in her ear. His fingers forced her chin up, and he said, 'Kiss me properly, like you did before.' His mouth teased her, and his fingers slid around to her nape, jerking up into the unbound thickness of her hair, which the slipping shawl had uncovered. His other hand was, unthinkably, stroking her breast through the woollen nightgown she had saved so hard to purchase for the voyage. 'Put your arms about me, so,' he draped her arms about his neck and held her

fast against him. 'Very good, Miss Banister,' he
mocked.

She opened her mouth to call him something she
had heard one of the workhouse girls call the
fish-boy, but he stopped her with another kiss. For
a moment she felt as though her insides were
molten and there was a shaft of intense delight.
Was she after all as weak-willed as Jane? she
thought with real despair, her life-long principles
melting like butter about her. She had considered
herself far above such things as bodily delights, and
here she was swooning from a kiss in the arms of a
handsome, feckless lecher!

'Please,' she whispered, tears stinging her eyes.
He stiffened at the sound of the word, and held her
a little away so that the saloon light fell on her
features. She felt him study her, though she dared
not meet his gaze. It sounded almost as if he sighed,
but the next moment he was as sarcastic as ever,
disabusing her mind of the idea he might be regretting his actions.

'Psst, you're too thin, Miss Banister! You need to
put on flesh.'

She pulled away, the spark of rage bringing her
back to life. He watched her, and his mouth twisted
in laughter. 'Leave me alone,' she began, not for a
moment expecting him to.

'As you will,' he bowed slightly. 'Thank you for
your company, Miss Banister. I have enjoyed it . . .
very much.'

He was gone before she realised it, leaving her
very confused and ashamed. The stars above mocked her, and her cheeks burned. She put cold hands
to them, biting her lips. What in God's name had
got into her to behave so . . . so wantonly? She
must be feverish, it was the only explanation. And

contradictorily, how dared he suddenly decide she was too thin and leave her like that?

Jane was still not back when Lizzie lay down on her bunk, and she was almost glad to be alone. She pressed her cheek to her hand, going over and over what had happened. How could she, Lizzie Banister, have allowed herself to be . . . to be fondled by that man? She bit her lip, blocking the memories, and almost cried out when Jane tapped her arm.

'Lizzie? Are you ill?'

'No, I . . . I . . .' Lizzie sat up, all personal thoughts flying from her mind as she glared at the dark silhouette of her sister. 'Where were you, Miss?'

Jane stepped back from the sharpness of Lizzie's voice, and several women close by shushed her. 'I was walking,' she whispered back, 'and thinking. What did you think I was doing?' she added shrewdly, and Lizzie was silent. Jane came closer, 'I can look after myself, Lizzie,' she said gently. 'And make up my own mind about . . . things.'

Lizzie felt her breath go out in relief. Her sister was not so easily led after all! She need not have gone so foolishly to her rescue, she need not have gone through that experience with that man. 'All right,' she said, 'go to sleep.'

But Lizzie lay awake for a long time, remembering. In fact, her head ached with remembering, and she closed her eyes at last, listening to the creak and groan of the ship's timbers.

She woke next morning to a headache and dark circled eyes. Jane dragged her out into the fresh air, and she went reluctantly. She didn't want to see that man, but she knew it would be equally ridiculous to lurk below decks until they made land. She must act as if nothing had happened, as if it meant nothing. Unless of course he had told others! She pushed the horror of that aside. He could not do so without making himself look as ridiculous as she.

The weather was perfect, and the blue sky lifted her spirits somewhat. Jane went with some of the younger girls to watch as the mariners caught flying fish, and Lizzie sat alone, eyes closed, letting the usual sounds wash about her.

'Miss Banister.'

She turned, frowning furiously. Humour shone in his eyes, and mockery. He sat down beside her, and she shifted away like a scalded cat. The laughter gleamed, so that he veiled his eyes with dark lashes. 'Miss Banister, you look rather flushed. Are you well?'

He observed the colour come into her pale cheeks, and the indignation of her gasp. 'I am perfectly well!'

His gaze took in her face with leisurely pleasure. 'You are really quite striking,' he said at last, as though surprised he should find it so. 'Not in the ordinary way at all. If you were to leave those drab gowns and wear something with a little more colour in it. I can see you in pale blue silk, lying back among cushions, with feathers—'

She stood up, trembling with a mixture of rage and fright. 'I don't wish to hear any more!'

He bit his lips, and stood up to face her. 'Miss Banister, forgive me. I digress. I sought you out this morning because I wanted to offer you my assistance.'

She was surprised, and suspicious. He saw both in her eyes, and his mouth twitched with laughter. 'You surprise me,' she said, forcing the usual calm into her voice.

'What did you expect me to do? Inform the entire ship?'

He saw in her eyes that he was correct, and the humour was suddenly gone. 'You have a fine opinion of me, I see,' he murmured briskly, and she realised with some amazement that he was actually hurt. 'Well, the truth is, Miss Banister, I wished to offer you my help. I have some influence in Sydney Town, and if you are looking for work there I can do my best to get you some.'

'I'll bet you can.'

He looked grim, and angry. 'I assure you I am not offering you a dishonourable proposal. You are hardly the sort of woman I would wish to keep.' He watched with satisfaction as the insult registered and the colour left her cheeks. They stared at each other like two cats, fur bristling, backs arched.

'Work is not so easy to come by as you may have imagined,' he added in milder tones. 'And I don't often feel the urge to be the author of an unselfish act. Don't deny me this one.'

Lizzie scowled at him, and her voice was thick with malicious pleasure. 'I wouldn't take water from you, Mr Gray, even if I were dying of thirst, so there! Take your job and . . . and . . . I want nothing further to do with you, ever!'

His lips thinned, and he looked at her with hard, black eyes. She lifted her chin, daring him to plead, to say anything in his defence. And then he bowed once, briskly, and said as if to a complete stranger, 'Very well. I wish you luck. And one more thing . . .' black eyes flickered with his own malicious need to wound, '. . . remember me when you're alone in your bed, Miss Banister, and how you enjoyed it!'

Hatred surged through her, but she said nothing

as he turned and walked away. It wasn't true of course; he'd said it because she had rebuffed him. It didn't mean a thing. If she kept repeating that to herself, she may just come to believe it.

She had always prided herself on being such a sensible, calm woman. The perfect, efficient lady's maid; a background shadow. Now, suddenly, she had been forced out into the light, blinking against the glitter of hard reality. He had shown her of what she might be capable, and it frightened her. Frightened her, too, that she could act so with a man she had claimed to loathe; a self-confessed rake with no morals and no principles whatsoever. His pretence at helping her find work she dismissed at once as some devious plot to bring her to her knees. She had won that round, anyway. Why did she feel, then, as if the game were not over?

CHAPTER
THREE

THEY reached land less than a week later. Lizzie
had never been so glad of anything in her life. The
other women seemed glad too, and Jane, though
quieter these days, ran to the railing with the rest of
them to watch as the *Governor* made her stately
way through the heads of Sydney Harbour, and
passed by the many jutting points of land, and
multitudes of secluded coves, before finally
reaching the wharves of Sydney Cove.

It bustled with life, people everywhere, and behind them the warehouses and dockside inns, the
cottages and the merchants' mansions. There was a
windmill high up on a hill, and seagulls whirled and
cried like deserted children. Trees and other green-
ery covered some of the further reaches of land
butting into the harbour, which was blue, sparkling
with sunshine, a twin for the sky above. The breeze
brought with it new smells and tantalising aromas,
and Lizzie felt her spirits rise for the first time in
many days.

Jane saw her smile and hugged her suddenly
close to her own breast. 'Oh Lizzie, we're here!'

People had already begun disembarking. There
were some porters on the wharf and vehicles for
hire. A group of men were offering employment to
the bounty girls, and Jane and Lizzie hurried to get
down and beat the others to what was available.

But by the time they had reached the men, what

jobs were vacant had been taken. They were pushed and shoved by the swelling crowd, and in the end huddled back against some casks out of the way. Jane's eyes were monstrous as she watched the seamen and the ships against the blue harbour background. A gang of convicts was engaged in moving some crates, and when one offered Jane an indecent proposal, Lizzie decided it was time to leave the docks behind, fascinating as they were.

They wandered up into the township, carrying their bags as best they could. The cottages and taverns were crowded together along narrow streets, and unsavoury characters watched the two girls pass. But gradually the streets grew wider, and the houses more respectable, and the passers-by too caught up in their own affairs to pay them much attention at all.

Jane paused to mop her brow, looking about her at the carts and carriages. A chain gang was working on the side of the roadway, and they skirted them gingerly. There were soldiers parading outside a red brick barracks, and cabbages growing in an extensive garden. Some of the houses were quite elegant, and a number had beautiful grounds—the ex-convict classes vying with the free classes in the bitter determination to show who was the better man.

Lizzie's bag was weighing heavily on her thin arms, and she and Jane paused to purchase bread and cheese to munch on while they surveyed the scene. It was early afternoon already, and they had to find lodgings for the night.

'Are you ill?'

Lizzie looked up to find her sister frowning at her. 'Ill, no, tired, yes. Oh Jane, I didn't think it would be so difficult! I was a fool to believe all they said in those posters.'

Jane shrugged, 'We've only asked at about ten shops. There's lots more, and they all look prosperous. Lots of houses, too. We'll find something, don't worry.'

They looked at each other, both thinking it strange to have changed roles so. Lizzie sighed. She did feel odd. Dizzy and hot, and cold too. One of the other women had been feeling feverish these past days, but had not asked the doctor for medication in case they refused to let her ashore. Lizzie, sorry for her, had helped her to be comfortable. She swallowed, and pushing her own ills aside, smiled at Jane.

'At least we've money for a few days,' she said.

They wandered aimlessly along the street. Lizzie was remembering Hezekiah Gray's offer of work, and suddenly she wondered if she had done the right thing in refusing. And yet how could she accept after what he had said, and done? It would mean burying her pride, and treating him as if he were *not* a rake, to be distrusted and disliked. She had caught sight of him when they were disembarking. He had been with Jason Wilson, and the two men had stood a while on the wharf, talking. She had watched him for some minutes before she became aware of the fact that she *was* watching him, and turned away. She had seen him on board ship, of course, during the final days, but he had not spoken to her and, as far as she knew, neither had he spoken to Jane. She thought of him now, and the picture was so clear and keen she jumped as if he had appeared at her side.

'Lizzie, you are ill! I told you not to go near that woman—'

'No, no,' she swallowed and brushed back a strand of dark hair from her forehead. 'Look, here's a laundry. We'll ask in here.'

The woman eyed them with sympathy. 'I'm sorry, lassie, there's nought for you here. My advice is to get back on the boat and go home. There's girls arriving every day, and there's not near enough work for them all. The ship owners are only interested in the bounty—they don't care what happens to the girls. And, life being what it is, most of the poor lassies end up on the streets. And I don't mean taking a morning stroll!'

Jane's eyes grew large. 'We can't go home!' she cried. 'Our money went on coming out here.'

The woman shrugged. 'I can't help you, love. I'm sorry, but there it is.'

They turned out of the steamy, hot interior, dragging their feet. Jane wiped a tear from her cheek, suddenly more frightened than she had been in many years. 'Oh Liz,' she breathed, 'what'll happen to us if there's no work?'

'Don't talk nonsense,' Lizzie snapped. 'We'll find work.'

Hezekiah's offer came to her again, plummeting her spirits. If they starved—for the alternative was impossible—it would be her fault, the fault of her own stubborn pride. If only . . .

A voice hailed them. They turned in surprise, as a youngish man stepped up to them, doffing his dusty hat, eyes shifting from Jane to Lizzie and back again.

''Scuse me ladies,' he said, 'but I heard you talking in there, and . . .' he cocked his head to one side. 'Well, I'm looking for a girl meself to help me at me work. I bought an inn, a few mile up the road from here. And not being married, you see, I need a girl to help like. What do you say? I'm offering free lodgings and food, in return for a bit of help about the place.'

The two girls looked at each other. Jane eyed him speculatively. 'One girl, you said?'

'Aye, well for the moment I've no need of two.'

'I'm not leaving me sister,' Jane said belligerently.

The hat was twisted between his fingers. He was only slightly taller than Lizzie, with sandy hair and a bony, nervous face. Yet his smile was gentle, and he seemed so anxious to please. 'Well, I don't know . . .'

Jane tilted her head, and smiled. 'Please,' she said.

His own lips quirked, and they looked at each other consideringly. 'You drive a hard bargain, don't you?'

Jane smiled. 'I do!'

'Very well.' The man's thin face broke into an ear-to-ear grin. 'Put your trust, girls, in Johnny Duff.'

'Mr Duff,' Lizzie said, stepping forward. 'It's very kind of you, however—'

Jane pulled her aside, her pretty face taut with the need to win her case. 'Don't you dare put him off,' she hissed. 'Don't you dare, Lizzie! We'll have free board and free food, and why, if we don't like it we can leave. We have to go somewhere, and this is as good an offer as any. Besides . . . I like him.'

Lizzie sniffed, but her head was aching abominably, and she knew she had no choice. Jane took the sniff as capitulation, and returned to Johnny Duff with a smile. 'It's all right,' she said.

Lizzie fixed him with a considering look. 'What's this inn called?'

He winked at her. 'The Thirsty Felon, I've called it. What do you think of that?'

Jane giggled. 'I think it's a wonderful name!'

Lizzie turned away so they wouldn't see her dismay. It was a far cry from all her dreams, but they had little choice, at least, for the moment. She sighed, and picking up her bag, followed Johnny Duff. He and Jane walked together, chattering as easily as if they had known each other all their lives. Lizzie envied them. She wished she could lift her spirits as easily, but they seemed very low at the moment. She wished, too, she felt less ill. It was hardly the moment to be getting feverish.

Johnny Duff had a dray, and helped them up on to the seat, tossing their bags into the back where he had a number of barrels, sacks and various odds and ends underneath a tarpaulin.

'How far is this inn?' Lizzie muttered.

He smiled, as he jerked the reins to gee up the old horse, and they moved jerkily off into the other traffic heading out of Sydney Town. 'A few mile up the road. Tell me, how was the voyage, ladies? I can see you're new chums.'

'New what?' Jane laughed.

'New chums. New to the colony, I mean.'

Jane chattered as they went, while Lizzie watched the passing scenery to ignore the bone-shaking jolt and rattle of the wooden dray. Her head was splitting so, she longed for nothing more than a dark room and a soft bed.

It seemed in no time at all they had left the bustle behind and were passing through the toll-bar into the surrounding countryside. A little way further on, and fields of wheat and corn stretched away to either side, broken by fields of pasture dotted with sheep. There were large homesteads, with larger gardens and orchards. They passed through one or two wayside townships, with mills by the river and stone cottages. Bush, too, quiet and rather intimidating to one used to the thick populace of London.

Lizzie dozed, head drooping towards her chest, and when she woke it seemed to her they had been travelling a very long time. The sky was turning to pink and mauve, and she shaded her eyes against the dying sun. The road stretched on, the bush hemmed them in. 'How far is it for God's sake!' she demanded.

Johnny Duff looked hurt. 'A few mile. Nearly there, ladies, never fear. Johnny Duff's a man of his word.'

Jane giggled, and Lizzie looked at her with a resigned sigh. She was in love again, and their feet were hardly dry from the ship. It had often amazed her how often Jane fell in and out of love, and it annoyed her a little, for she had never considered herself in love at all. Not even once. 'Love is for common folk,' the old cook used to say to her. 'To get on in the world's more important than bodily matters.' And Lizzie, remembering the stolen passageway kiss, had flushed to the roots of her curling hair.

'Here we are!'

She came out of her reverie at the sound of his voice, looking about her a little dazedly. The 'inn' was a hut, made of split timber logs and roofed with slabs of bark, broken only by a cask fashioned into a makeshift chimney. There was a window, covered with fastened wooden shutters, and a trough and hitching rail. A roughly-painted sign was displayed proudly above the door, depicting a wretch with ball and chain fastened to one ankle who was drinking from a tankard. Behind the hut another building loomed, with large doors. The stable, no doubt.

'What do you think then?' Johnny Duff demanded, attempting to hide the pride in his voice.

Jane caught Lizzie's eye, both girls looking a little bewildered. 'Well,' Jane said gently, 'I think it remarkable, sir.'

'I think you did right in employing two women,' Lizzie muttered cryptically, and Johnny looked at her with some uncertainty. He jumped down to the ground. Jane took his hand with a smile, and hopped down beside him. Lizzie came more slowly, resting a moment against the wheel to ease her aching head. She shivered, rubbing her hands over her arms, watching as the other two began to unload the dray.

'Come on, ladies. Come inside, and I'll see to old Ned here.'

Inside, the hut was sparsely furnished—a few shelves, and a bench, with a table by the fireplace. A doorway curtained with some yellowing material led through to a makeshift bedroom. The bed itself was a platform covered in bark with two blankets, one for beneath and one for above. A log of wood wrapped in more yellowing cloth was the pillow. Lizzie leaned against the jamb, feeling close to tears. Why, oh why hadn't she swallowed her pride and agreed to Hezekiah Gray's offer?

But Jane was already putting their bags in and spreading out their own blankets. She was even humming under her breath, and Lizzie wondered suspiciously if she had gone mad. If love was such a tonic for the mind and body, perhaps Cook had been wrong?

'I mean to build more, of course,' Johnny said from the other room. They could hear him heaving the purchases about. 'But this will do for the moment. You ladies can have that room. I'll kip in the stables.'

'Oh Jane,' Lizzie whispered, when he had gone. 'We're miles from anywhere.'

'There must be people,' Jane said. 'An inn has to have customers.'

'I get lots of folk in here, you know.' Johnny was back again, as if reading their minds. 'Folk on their way to Bathurst, over the Blue Mountains. Not too many places along this stretch of road for a man to quench his thirst.'

They went out into the other room, where he was mopping his brow. He eyed Lizzie doubtfully. Jane dimpled, and he turned to her with some relief. Here was someone he understood, here was someone he could talk to. He had done right in bringing Jane.

They ate a meal of stew, followed by bread cooked in the ashes of the fire, and afterwards warm, bitter tea. Lizzie couldn't seem to swallow much of hers, and didn't argue when Jane sent her to her bed. She was asleep almost at once, but not a restful sleep. It was filled with faces and black eyes, and the feel of strong arms binding her close. She did not hear Jane slide into bed beside her, and did not even think to worry for her.

Morning found her unrested, and dizzy when she tried to stand. Neither of the girls had undressed, and Lizzie lay back, trying to still the throbbing in her head. Her throat felt sore and dry, and she swallowed carefully.

She felt a tremor of fear. The memory of her illness two years ago was suddenly clear in her mind. She had almost died then of a fever and if she had not been strong of body and will she would certainly have died in the workhouse. If she died now, Jane would be alone, with no one to care for her. She could not bring her sister all these thousands of miles and then die on her, could she?

'And who ever said anything about dying?' she retorted loudly, and tried to force unwilling legs out of bed. She clung a moment to the door jamb, getting her breath.

In the other room, Johnny had started a fire in the big hearth, and the flames made the place almost cheerful. He smiled up at Lizzie, and Jane looked up from her place beside him, blue eyes dancing. 'Lizzie, Mr Duff has so many plans. You wouldn't believe—' she stopped, frowning at her sister. 'You look tired. Sit here and I'll tend to breakfast.'

Johnny winked as she sat down stiffly beside him. 'Your sister is a right bossy piece. I've been told cooking is woman's work. Wish I'd had someone to tell me that this year past!'

Lizzie forced a smile, and watched covertly as he set about lacing up his boots. He was not a handsome boy, but there was humour in his features, and something of strength and determination in the line of his mouth and jaw. His hair was an uncompromising ginger, and lank, but looked clean. She let her glance slide to Jane, and studied her too for a moment.

'Here we are!'

Jane placed the egg and fried bread in front of her. Lizzie stared at it, willing her stomach to quieten. After a moment, she pushed it away and said, in a shaking voice, 'I think I'm going to be ill. Perhaps you'd excuse me.'

Jane found her beneath a tree, resting her forehead to the trunk and feeling sorry for herself. The younger girl bit her lips, terror for a moment making her mind blank. Lizzie had been so ill, that time in the workhouse. They had thought she would die. And now she was ill again, and they were alone out here in the bush with no one to help and she didn't know what to do. It took considerable will-power to steady her hands, and she went forward briskly.

'Lizzie, you should have stayed in bed. Come now . . '

Lizzie leaned against her, seeming not to know for a moment who she was. Jane looked up in relief when Johnny appeared. 'What shall I do?' she whispered, blue eyes filled with sudden tears. Johnny felt his heart melt at the sight of her brave, lovely smile.

'Don't fret,' he said, trying for a brisk note. 'Just take her in and make her comfortable.'

When Jane reappeared Johnny was staring down at his boots. He pulled a face when he saw her. 'You want a doctor, I suppose, Jane. The thing is . . . there's not one around here. I'll have to go into Sydney Town, and then like as not no doctor'll come out here unless he's paid more than he should be. I haven't got that kind of money.'

Jane's eyes blurred with more tears. 'What else can we do!'

He sighed. 'Aye, well I can try. And while I'm there I'll visit the apothecary and see about some medicine for her.'

Jane put her hand on his arm, squeezing it warmly. 'You're a good man, Johnny Duff,' she whispered. He paused, looking down at her, and then suddenly stooped and kissed her lips. He was gone before she could do more than touch the spot with her own fingers. It was a far different kiss than any she had had before, certainly any she had had from

Zek Gray. There was no artifice about Johnny, what you saw was what there was. For the last time in her life, Jane Banister fell in love.

The day dragged endlessly into evening. Jane swept out the tap-room as best she could—the floor was of hardpacked earth—in between going in to Lizzie to mop her face with cool water, and try to get her to drink. She was burning, and tossing so violently on occasions that Jane struggled to hold her down. Her breathing was harsh, and once she cried out. Jane watched her constantly after that, but as evening drew in Lizzie fell frighteningly quiet and lay still, only the sound of her breathing breaking the stillness of the room. Outside, crickets sang a constant chorus, and the bush lay dark and strange. Jane had never felt quite so lonely in her life.

Jane had dozed off herself when she heard the horse. It drew closer, and just as she imagined it would pass by the pattern of hoof beats altered. The animal snorted, jingling its reins. Thinking it was Johnny returned at last, she ran out into the darkness, snatching up the whale-oil lantern.

She saw the horse, standing quiet, and looked wildly around for its rider. He came from the side, a dark silhouette, and she saw at once he was not Johnny. A taller man, and more thick-set. For a moment he seemed terribly familiar, and then, as he came into the circle of light, she recognised him.

'Mr Gray!' her breath caught, and her heart thumped unpleasantly. The black eyes widened in surprise, and then he was smiling.

'Jane Banister, as I live and breathe!'

'I . . .' she began, and glanced over her shoulder. 'Oh Mr Gray, me sister's ever so sick!' The tears came pouring down her cheeks. 'She just lies there, and . . . and I don't know what to do. She's the one who always knows what to do, and she was awful sick before and . . . and I think she's going to die!'

'Hush,' he said sternly, and for a moment considered her white face with its huge, dark-shadowed eyes. 'I stopped for a drink,' he added quietly, 'before continuing on my way to Bathurst. Can you get me a drink, Jane, while I take a look at your sister?'

Jane nodded, wiping her cheeks, and went in to fetch his drink.

Hezekiah Gray followed her, and went through into the other room. There was a candle near the bed, already burnt well down. The woman was lying under a blanket, quite still, her face like alabaster beneath dark, irrepressible hair. He thought for a moment it was too late already, until he saw the way her hands clenched and unclenched on the blankets. He covered them with his own. Her flesh was dry and burning.

'Well,' he murmured, his expression unreadable as he looked down at her, 'this is what you've come to, Miss Lizzie Banister.'

At the sound of her name she stirred a little, and the incredibly thick eyelashes swept up. Her eyes gleamed, but in a blurred way. She licked her lips, and tried to speak, but her voice was a mere croak. She licked her lips again, and looking around he saw a jug of water and poured some into a glass. He lifted her, holding her upright against him as she drank. The effort seemed to exhaust her, and she lay back down with a soft groan.

'Lizzie Banister?' he whispered, and brushed her dark hair back from her forehead. It was soft as silk, for all its riotous curl, and his hand trembled a little.

Lizzie, struggling against a world of darkness and death, felt his hand and heard his voice, and something in both prodded the old fighting spirit back to life. 'I'm not dying,' she said harshly.

'Well of course you're not, Lizzie Banister!' He put his finger on her lips, tracing their outline, and her eyes gazed up at him in a sort of baffled wonder. 'I think, first of all, we should break that fever of yours,' he said, 'and then we'll see about getting you on to your feet again.'

Jane appeared behind him with a tankard, and he took it with a smile and drank.

'Is she . . .' Jane managed, but he shook his head.

'No more weeping,' he said sternly. 'We have work to do.'

Lizzie, hovering between reality and delirium, remembered vague bits and pieces—being stripped down to her shift by a pair of firm masculine hands, and then covered with blankets until she perspired freely. She cried out, trying to escape the offending hands, but they held her firm. The devil seemed to have arrived to torment her, and no matter how she tried to escape him, he would not leave her alone.

'Drink this, Lizzie, or I'll have to hold your nose until you do.'

She opened her eyes to glare at him, and saw how tired he looked, his shirt unbuttoned and his hair untidy and damp from the heat. Black eyes mocked her, unfathomable as the deepest ocean, and she gazed into them. Her mouth began to tremble with weakness, and a tear ran down her cheek.

'Don't let me die,' she said shakily.

He was staring at her, and suddenly stooped and put his mouth against her own soft lips.

'I won't let you die now, Lizzie,' he whispered. 'Only saints die young,' and he grinned into her furious eyes.

'How do you know I'm not?' she hissed.

'A saint? Oh, Lizzie!'

He lifted her up, so that she could drink the warm broth. She took several mouthfuls before she shook her head. He put the bowl down, lowering her gently back on to the bed. For a moment he looked at her, expressionless. Her eyelashes flickered, sweeping her cheeks.

'How did you find us?' she said at last. The fact that he was here had not struck her as odd while she was so ill, but now, with her mind weary but clear, she thought it very odd indeed.

He smiled. 'I was riding out to Bathurst. I have to get back to my farm. I stopped for a drink.'

Her eyes flickered again, and this time stayed closed. Her breathing slowed and deepened. After a moment he rose, and was at the door when Jane entered.

'I've heated water if you wish to wash,' she whispered. 'And Johnny's back. He's brought some medicine, but no doctor.'

Hezekiah Gray smiled. 'No matter. The fever's broken and she's sleeping normally. I'm starving, by the way.'

She smiled. 'Johnny's tending to that, Mr Gray. I'll just sit by Lizzie a while. And Mr Gray . . . thank you, very much.'

He flicked her cheek with his finger, and left her.

Jane sat down by Lizzie's bed, deep in thought. She had looked in earlier, unbeknown to Zek Gray, and had seen him kiss her. Lizzie and Mr

Gray! It seemed preposterous, and yet . . . Sighing, she rearranged her sister's blankets, and settled to wait.

CHAPTER
FOUR

'LIZZIE?' Jane's cool hand on her brow. She smiled up at her sister's drawn, anxious face. For a moment it hovered on the brink of tears, and then Jane broke into a beaming smile. 'Oh Lizzie, I'm so glad you're well again!'

'Johnny?'

'He's sleeping. He couldn't find anyone to come, and he was so upset.' Her blue eyes were tender. 'Are you hungry? We've had our breakfast long ago. It's almost noon, you know.'

'I'm thirsty, that's all.'

'Mr Gray has some brandy he said you're to take with water.'

'Indeed!'

Jane bit her lip. 'I know how you feel about him, Liz, but he's been so good, and I think he saved your life.'

Lizzie glared at her a moment, and then sighed. 'I wonder he bothered.'

'Liz, how can you be so ungrateful?' Jane whispered, and stalked out.

Lizzie closed her eyes. She was grateful to him of course, but she could hardly alter her opinion of him because of that, could she? And now that she came to recall their talk earlier, she seemed to remember him kissing her! How dared he take liberties with her weakness! Actually assaulting her when she was quite unable to defend herself! It only went to prove what an unscrupulous rake the man was.

A footstep in the doorway made her open her eyes. For a moment she thought . . . hoped, it was Johnny.

'Miss Banister?'

Johnny never spoke in that low, satyr's voice.

'Mr Gray.'

'Ah, you're sounding more like your old dis-approving self.'

He had washed and tidied his clothing, though he had left off his coat and unbuttoned his shirt half-way down his chest—both sins when visiting a sick-bed, in Lizzie's eyes. That he looked very handsome was no excuse and certainly of no merit. She watched him distrustfully as he came closer, and put his palm on her forehead.

Black eyes danced down at her, the lines on his face deepening with laughter. Lines of dissipation, Lizzie thought darkly. Any man with such know-ing, wicked eyes and such a cynical, world-weary smile must be dissipated.

'Must you frown like that, Lizzie?' the low voice mocked her. 'It's hideous.'

She scowled even more blackly. He sighed. 'Back to normal, are we? Well I've wasted quite enough time on you. I've my own business to attend to.'

As he turned away, she was struck with remorse. He *had* saved her life. And even lechers should be given thanks where thanks were due.

'Mr Gray?'

He looked at her over his broad shoulder, eye-brows raised with mock inquiry.

'I'm . . . well, I'm sorry. Thank you for what you did.'

She was flushing like a child! She wished she didn't have to lie there so much at a disadvantage. Jane had put her in a clean shift with a rather lower neckline than she liked, and she pulled the blanket up to her chin. He noticed the gesture and his mouth quirked.

'There's really no need for such modesty, Miss Banister. You've got nothing there I didn't become familiar with last night. And if I'd had intentions of forcing myself on you, God forbid, I could have done so then.'

He was laughing at her. 'What do you mean?' she whispered, brown eyes wide.

'Who do you think washed you to keep your temperature down? Good fairies? And who was it stripped you of those rags you persist in wearing?'

'You didn't!'

But now that she thought about it, she remembered his hands, and knew that he spoke the truth. The colour flooded her face like a spring tide, and she bit her lip, staring at him over the blanket, shock and anger struggling for supremacy. He grinned at her, the wicked light dancing in his eyes.

'Who'd have thought it?' he mused, enjoying her discomfort. 'Without your clothes, Lizzie Banister, you're rather lovely. And believe me, I'm an expert on the subject.'

For a moment she stuttered, unable to think of anything bad enough to call him. He watched her in amusement, bold black eyes raking her covered form.

'How dared you?' she whispered, choking on humiliation and indignation.

An eyebrow quirked. 'Would you have preferred I let you die? What odd rules our society has,

Lizzie, when it is better for a maiden to die than be seen without her clothes!'

'You don't understand,' she said darkly.

But he laughed, tossing over his shoulder, 'Goodbye, Lizzie. I fear we *shall* meet again.'

She lay a moment, numb with the thought of him touching her . . . bathing her, until she realised her genuine horror was mixed with a sort of excitement that frightened her even more. Impure thoughts! Cook had warned her about them. A girl must be pure, modest and behave with circumspection in all matters. She must not associate with men of loose morals, and if she should be unlucky enough to come into contact with one of the creatures, she should be polite but cool and never, never put herself into a position where she might be taken advantage of.

Lizzie bit her lip nervously. Was it her fault she had fallen ill and been forced to depend upon Zek Gray? She had a feeling that Cook would think so, and Cook was her doyenne in such matters. And yet, wouldn't it be uncharitable not to be grateful towards him? She sighed suddenly. It was all too much, and besides . . . she probably would never see him again, despite that cryptic farewell of his.

She slept, and continued to sleep much of the next day, eating and then sleeping again. It wasn't until the following day that Jane told her Zek Gray had gone.

'But he promised to come by in a couple of weeks. To see how you were, he said.' Jane eyed her sister's heightened colour speculatively. 'He said you're as strong as a horse . . . a mule he said, rather, and that you'll soon be up again.'

Lizzie narrowed her eyes. 'Did he indeed!'

Jane bit back a smile. He had certainly put the

life back into her sister. And yet he wasn't remotely loverlike in his actions towards her; not at all as he had acted towards Jane herself, when he was working towards the big seduction. After the kiss she'd witnessed Jane had expected more of the same, but all she had heard were insults and mockery, designed to send Lizzie's starched morals into fits. How strange that someone as sensual and experienced as Zek Gray should be attracted to her plain-speaking, uncompromising, yes, *puritan* sister! But perhaps it was that very fact that attracted him. He would find Lizzie quite a new experience, after the flirts and the misses who flung themselves at his head, ripe and ready for seduction.

As the days passed Lizzie grew stronger, and was soon up and about, getting under Jane's feet. Quite a few travellers stopped at the tavern, and Jane had quickly got into the way of exchanging quips and comments, making them welcome. Johnny was always there to see they didn't consider her charms part and parcel of the service, and noting the protective way he stood by her, Lizzie had begun to wonder if there wasn't more than friendship between them.

There was a town called Evanstown about an hour's ride up the Bathurst road, and Johnny took them there one morning. A few cottages and a tavern—which Johnny dismissed as second-rate—but little more than that. A struggling English seedling in the midst of the alien Australian bush, or that was how Lizzie thought of it, gazing about at the blatantly English air of the place. On the way back Johnny frightened them with tales of bushrangers.

'Mostly convicts who've bolted and turned to thieving for a living,' he said, urging Old Ned into a trot. 'There's been some bad ones, I can tell you! One family a few mile up the road were murdered a few years ago; and then there was a woman kidnapped over Penrith way. Of course, in the end, the soldiers usually catch 'em, or shoot 'em dead.'

Jane shuddered, and pressed closer to his side. 'How horrible! I hope none decide to come to The Thirsty Felon, Johnny.'

He looked at her with warm, smiling eyes. 'If they do, Jane, I'll protect you. I'm a dab-hand with a gun meself, you know.'

'Oh?' Lizzie decided it was time for a change of subject, and, glancing uneasily over her shoulder resolutely set about it. 'Were you in the army then, Mr Duff?'

He looked at her, his face quite old suddenly. His pale eyes flickered away, and for a moment he stared over Ned's ears. 'No, Miss Lizzie, I weren't a soldier. I come out here under Government Orders.'

Then, when she smiled blankly, 'You don't know what I mean, do you? I was transported, ma'am. A convict. I stole some fruit from the barrow I was working and was caught. I got seven years. When I got here I was with the Government gang first, carrying stuff from the wharves, you know. Later I got consigned down the Hawksbury River way. A fair master, he was. I got my ticket a year after, and my pardon a year after that. I worked on there for two more years, saving my money, until I bought this place. I reckon a little while more, and I'll be spreadin' out, no worries.'

There was a silence. Johnny had kept talking in his slow, easy voice. Perhaps he had realised they were shocked, and kept on until they were more used to the idea that he was an ex-convict. Jane swallowed, and after a moment rested her hand on his arm. He glanced at her, smiling, though his face was stiff, all the natural laughter gone out of him.

'It doesn't matter to me, Johnny,' she said gently. 'I've done things too, and . . . It just doesn't matter.'

'But Mr Duff . . . Johnny, if people know you're an . . . were a convict, won't they stay away from your drinking establishment?' Lizzie's wide eyes gazed into his.

For a moment he stared, and then chuckled at her unexpected naiviety.

'They can hardly do that,' he said, quite gently. 'A lot of the people we see have been convicts, or are ticket-of-leave men—or are married to convicts or their kids.'

'Ticket-of . . . ?'

'If a convict is well behaved, and does his work proper, he can apply for a "ticket", and that means he's free to find work on his own account. He has to take a certain Government-set wage, o' course. But he's free in the sense of not having any master.'

'You mean your customers . . . but not all of them surely!' Lizzie was appalled.

'New South Wales *is* a penal colony, Lizzie,' Jane retorted repressively. 'The first settlers were convicts. One must expect a certain percentage of the population to be convicts or their children.'

But Lizzie stared blindly at Johnnny, the idea of him being a criminal as yet totally unacceptable to her puritan ideals. Lizzie Banister was employed by a felon? Good Lord, no wonder he had called the place by that ridiculous name!

'Lizzie,' Jane hissed, watching the expressions flit over her sister's mobile features. 'What does it matter what Johnny was or is? He's been good to us, to you, and . . . and . . .' her eyes said the rest.

Johnny flicked her cheek with his finger, and smiled down at her warmly.

Lizzie's shoulders slumped. A felon in the family. Good God, what was the world coming to?

After that Lizzie began to take more note of the customers, eyeing them as though she would recognise a convict among them by some peculiarity. A striped skin perhaps, as Jane snapped.

There were a few small-holdings about them in the bush too, and those folk started to drop by, especially when they heard there were women to be seen. Jane seemed to enjoy having the company, and joined in the fun. Lizzie noticed, however, that she always kept her distance, and though she might flirt, it was not a serious sort of flirting. And she always included Johnny in the goings-on, turning to smile at him, or wink, or touch his arm. They were already a couple, and Lizzie knew it would only be a short while before her worst fears were confirmed.

What would Mama have said to having a felon in the family!

But more horrific still, what would *Cook* have said?

The two girls were stitching outdoors in the sunshine one afternoon some weeks later, when Jane settled the matter once and for all. She had been quiet for some time, and finally put her sewing aside altogether.

'Lizzie?'

'Hmm?' Lizzie's face had regained colour, and she looked relaxed and happy. The sun had tanned her skin too, taking away the usual matt white, bringing out red lights in her dark curls.

Jane smiled a little, as if remembering something

which pleased her. 'I meant to tell you before, but
. . . Lizzie, Johnny asked me to marry him. And I
want to, very much.'

Lizzie didn't speak for a moment, wondering
whether to be glad or sorry. Jane was a pretty girl;
she could have made a better match. And yet here
she was, considering marriage to a man who lived
miles from anywhere. And a felon to boot!

'Lizzie?'

Lizzie covered her sister's hand, her dark eyes
worried. 'If you mean to marry him Jane, I can
hardly prevent it. I only want you to be happy. But
surely . . . Oh Jane, he's not at all what I had
hoped!'

Jane's blue eyes gleamed with sudden anger.
'Because of what he was honest enough to tell us?
He needn't have, you know, Liz. He could have
kept his mouth shut, and we'd have never known,
would we? And so what? I've been to the House of
Correction myself, haven't I?'

'That's different!'

Jane drew back, and Lizzie saw two pink spots of
fury in her cheeks. Like a wild animal protecting
her mate, she thought wryly.

'I know you don't like him, Liz. I can't help that,
and I don't care much. I happen to love him. And
what of our dear father, Liz, what of him?'

'I *do* like him, I . . .' Lizzie frowned, puzzled.
'Pa? He died in an accident at the docks, you know
that!'

Jane shook her head slowly, and she looked
suddenly so much like their mother that Lizzie bit
her lip.

'No he didn't, Lizzie. Mama told me once, when
I was bad. I forget what I did, but Mama was upset
and she said I'd go the same way of me Da, and I

never forgot it, small as I was at the time. "You'll go bad like him", she said, "and they'll come and take you away, like him. And I'll never see you again outside bars, either".'

Lizzie had gone perfectly white. 'Oh Jane, don't.'

The two girls stared at each other.

'I'm sorry, but you were acting so lily-pure, and . . . we're no better than Johnny. He's good and kind and true, and no one can ask more of a man than that!'

Lizzie bowed her head, beaten. 'You've grown up,' she said. She was sad for it, though she knew the feeling to be wholly selfish. She had cared for Jane for so long, she felt that she would be rather at a loss without her there to boss and look after.

'I'll go and tell Johnny you agree to it,' Jane said, and was off to find him, skirts flying as she ran, blonde hair bouncing.

Lizzie watched her go, and foolishly wiped away a tear.

'Oh Mama,' she whispered, 'I never knew. Why didn't you say?'

But she knew why. Lizzie had been so respectable, and so proud of it, too. Lizzie would have been mortified at the knowledge, and Mama knew that. Working in that big, London town house had made her think she was a cut above the rest. Her mother had been so proud of her! Lizzie sighed.

Johnny came, plaiting his hat brim between dusty fingers.

'Lizzie.'

Jane stood behind him, gentle loving mockery in her eyes. She gave him a bit of a nudge, and Lizzie decided wryly that that was just what she would be doing for the rest of their lives together.

'Jane tells me you're agreeable to our wedding,' he said, pale eyes anxious. 'We want to marry as soon as practicable.'

'She has no dress, no . . . no . . .'

Jane made a face. 'Where would I get a weddin' dress from? And what would I pay for it with? And what on earth would I do with it afterwards?'

'But Mama always hoped . . . oh Jane, you know you look so lovely in white!'

Jane shrugged. 'That's as maybe,' she said practically, 'but it's not something that'll matter much. What matters is to be wed, and start building this place up, and being with Johnny.'

He looked at her, and Lizzie felt pain at the expression in his eyes. If only a man would look at her like that; as if she were the whole reason and delight of his life! She bit down on the thought and sighed. No man ever would; she was not the kind of girl for whom men formed unreasonable passions.

'Nothing I can say will make the slightest difference,' she said. 'So you may as well go ahead.'

Jane danced about a few steps in excitement. 'Johnny says there's a minister up at Evanstown, who has services in his house there. But we can get him down here to wed us. Oh Lizzie!'

Lizzie stood up. 'Well then, there's no time to waste, is there? We'll have to fix you up a dress, my girl, even if it's not a wedding dress, and see to supper for the guests and . . . There will be guests?'

Johnny nodded, smiling wryly. 'Aye, there will be. Everyone comes to a wedding.'

Jane's eyes shone. 'I never thought,' she said, 'when I came to Sydney Town, I'd meet my husband the very day I landed!'

After that the time flew. The minister was contacted, and during the intervening days Lizzie stitched to transform one of Jane's old gowns into something approaching beauty. There were flowers and lace for her hair, and more wild flowers to sew into the hem of her gown on the day. Lizzie cooked up a fine spread, with all the basics she could find. Whatever else went wrong, they would have enough to eat! Despite their hard work, it amazed her that everything was ready on the day. It seemed impossible that Jane was to be married, and to a . . . but she mustn't think of that! Jane to be married, and Lizzie bridesmaid, and so much to do.

Johnny rode out early to get the minister, and while he was gone Jane and Lizzie dressed and set up the tap-room as best they could with flowers and dried straw for the earth floor. When Jane was ready, Lizzie stood back to view her properly— pink gown, bright flowers sewn into it and worked into the girl's fair, shining hair.

'You look a treat,' she said softly, and patted her sister's hand.

'I feel so calm,' Jane murmured. 'I thought I would be all a-shake, but I'm so quiet and calm, Lizzie.'

'Well that's all to the good, love. Now hush, I hear someone coming. And for God's sake, don't go dragging out into the yard and getting yourself all dusty!'

She went outside, shading her eyes to the noon sun. A dark horse came around the corner, kicking up dust into the still air. The rider wore a black jacket and light breeches, with highly polished boots. No man of religion that she'd heard of would wear such boots!

'Miss Banister,' he said, halting only feet from where she stood. His horse stamped, and tossed its head, but Lizzie refused on principle to back away.

'Mr Gray,' she said politely, as if he were paying a call in London rather than the isolation of the Australian bush, and as if it hadn't been several weeks since she clapped eyes on his mocking, frighteningly handsome exterior.

'You're looking much better than when I last saw you,' he added, a distinct gleam in his black eyes.

His hair was windblown, and dusty, and dust layered his clothing, but he still contrived to look better than any man she had ever seen. Unconsciously she smoothed her clean skirts, and tucked in a stray curl where it had escaped the rigid *coiffure* she had affected for the wedding—until she realised what she was about and jerked her hands away.

'You're thinner than you should be, though,' he frowned, the lines on his face deepening. 'And I like you better with your hair loose.'

She realised then, with a start, that they had been staring at each other for some moments, reconfirming certain points and items of memory.

'Indeed! Perhaps you would care for a drink, Mr Gray. I should perhaps warn you, however, that my sister is being married as soon as the reverend arrives . . .'

He had dismounted, and had been searching in his saddle-bags for something, but now looked up with a faint smile. 'I did know, Miss Banister. Your sister wrote me a very neat little invitation, and I was fortunately able to accept. I left her my address, in case . . . well, just in case. Wonderful news, isn't it?'

'Your attendance or the wedding?'

'The wedding, of course.'

'Wonderful.' But she sounded sour. He narrowed his eyes at her.

'Aren't you going to ask me in?'

Whether she would have or not was debatable, but at that moment Jane appeared in her finery, and came hurrying towards him. 'Mr Gray! I'm so glad you came. You are to be our best man!'

He laughed his soft laugh, and caught her about the waist, stooping to kiss her cheek with a warmth Lizzie found rather obscene.

'I believe the best man has a right to kiss the bride,' he said, and Jane blushed. 'I've brought you a present, too.' He gave her the packet from his saddle-bag.

'Oh, thank you. But you must be thirsty! Lizzie, go and get Mr Gray a drink of our best ale, while I explain to him what he must do.'

Lizzie pulled a face and stomped inside. Once there, she took a number of deep breaths, telling herself she was a fool to be so upset by the sight of that handsome, experienced face. Why on earth had Jane invited him? But still, the damage was done. She must just avoid him as much as possible, and pray he didn't seek her out.

By the time she returned, the couple were seated on the bench outside, heads close. Jane took the tankard and handed it to Zek, smiling it seemed with an effort. He drank a good half before looking up at Lizzie.

'Thank you. I've ridden hard for quite a few hours to get here on time. I needed that.'

Jane stood up, shaking out her pink skirts. 'Excuse me,' she said, her face curiously expressionless, 'I have things to attend to.'

Lizzie glared at her, but Jane kept her face averted until she reached the tavern and disappeared inside. Gray was watching her when she turned back to him, a curiously searching expression in his eyes, and she frowned.

'What do you intend to do when they're married?' he asked softly.

She lifted her eyebrows at his presumption. 'I haven't thought about it,' she said coolly, thinking that that would put him in his place. In fact, she had thought of nothing else.

'You don't intend to stay here, surely,' he went on. 'Jane will need to be mistress of the house, and she can hardly be that with you lording it over everything.'

She flushed angrily. 'I hardly think that it concerns you!'

'No?' There was a pause while he looked down into the tankard, where he held it in laced fingers. 'I have a proposition to put before you, Miss Lizzie Banister.' She opened her mouth. 'And don't you dare say what you're going to say!'

She glared at him in silence, before he dropped his gaze once more to the tankard.

'I need someone to see to the house and generally look after me. A housekeeper, if you like. The position would be well paid, and though the conditions are probably not London town house standard, I'm sure you'll soon adapt to them.'

'Housekeeper!'

'Generally speaking, yes.'

'I should have thought you'd prefer someone more . . . willing to conform to your standards, Mr Gray.'

'Now what the devil is that supposed to mean?'

His anger shone clearly in his eyes, and for a moment she was startled by it. But she stood her ground, knowing she was in the right, and forced her voice to remain infuriatingly cool and calm.

'Mean? I thought that was obvious.'

'Miss Banister, you're clearly not needed here. You're looking for work and accommodation. I can offer both, and pay you for them. You have only to answer me yes or no.'

She bit her lip. Put like that it was almost tempting . . . and yet she must be a fool for contemplating such a thing. Why did the idea give her such a thrill of excitement? Perhaps because she knew it was a daring, un-cooklike thing to do. She loathed him and knew him for what he was, and yet . . . there was something about pitting her wits against his that made her feel more alive than she had in a long, long time.

'Can I give you my answer after the wedding?' she muttered gruffly.

'Of course,' he said, and smiled. It was too bland a smile, and mockery gleamed in his dark eyes. She glared back.

Jane was returning to join them, and the conversation was at an end. After a moment Johnny too arrived, with the minister in tow, and a number of other folk from Evanstown. All future thoughts were forgotten in the babble and bustle of the present. More guests began arriving, bringing their children with them. Lizzie found herself holding a baby, which dribbled on her shoulder and sobbed alarmingly when she smiled at it.

'You've such a way with children,' Zek Gray murmured in her ear.

He took the child from her, and minutes later it was laughing. Lizzie turned her back, and bent stiffly to handing around plates of cakes.

The ceremony went smoothly enough. Jane and Johnny stood together before the minister, and Lizzie and Zek stood behind. Lizzie found herself unaccountably tearful and once, when wiping her cheeks in a manner she thought surreptitious, turned to find him watching her. His face creased immediately into what she privately called 'the mocking look', and bending towards her he murmured, 'Never mind. You know what they say. First a bridesmaid, then a bride.'

Gazing stonily in front of her, she wondered what it was about him that seemed to bring out the worst feelings in her. Cook would have been amazed at the sheer savagery of her thoughts at this moment, for instance. Not like prim and proper Lizzie Banister at all.

The celebrations began the moment the minister had spoken the last words, and with a whoop the men began to claim kisses from the bride. Food was consumed, and drink was drunk. One of the guests had brought a jew's harp, and they danced to that with much enthusiasm if little expertise. There wasn't much room, and a lot of the merriment spilled outside into the moonlight.

Jane, flushed and beautiful, danced with them all. The straw and dust kicked up by their feet was choking, and Lizzie, sitting by the wall, foot tapping under cover of her skirts, found herself sneezing with the rest. She watched in some disgust as Zek Gray joined in the dancing, partnering the women and enjoying himself quite unselfconsciously. Trust him to make a fool of himself, Lizzie thought smugly, and concentrated on being above such common things.

The man was a flirt. Just look at the way he was speaking to that red head! Black eyes bold as brass, and the very way he smiled was indecent. There he stood, completely at ease; a teasing, laughing heart-breaking devil!

He and Jane danced, and finished with much

laughter. Then Johnny claimed her, holding her close, and by the ecstatic look on her sister's face Lizzie knew this dance meant more than all the rest. She was torn between gladness and sorrow. Jane had not made a good marriage, in the social sense, and yet . . . 'good' marriages were often hell to the parties concerned. She sighed, the problem too great for her tired brain.

She had closed her eyes momentarily, but the presence of someone standing over her was so oppressive, she opened them with a start, finding herself looking straight up into those only too familiar bold ones.

'Dance, Miss Banister?' he said softly, and held out his hand.

She eyed it with misgivings.

'I consider dancing undignified,' she told him sternly, smoothing her skirts of imaginary wrinkles. 'But thank you for asking, Mr Gray.' If he were a gentleman, she thought, that would be the end of the matter.

She dared a glance through her lashes and saw that his eyes had gone quite cool. Next thing he had caught her arm and was heaving her to her feet. Someone laughed, and another cheered. Lizzie struggled in mortification, but he pulled her against him, sliding his arms about her to hold her still. His quiet voice whispered into her ear, sending shivers up and down her spine.

'You'll dance, Lizzie Banister, or I'll turn you over my knee . . .'

Her head went back, and she stared into his admittedly beautiful eyes. 'I'll never forgive you for this,' she hissed. 'Never!'

He laughed as he swung her around, pulling her back hard against his body, and she found her feet forced to follow the rhythm of his, her skirts swirling with every turn and twist.

'No gentleman would hold a lady so close,' she gasped, when his hand spread over the small of her back. She could feel every wrinkle of his clothing, every muscle of his body, and . . . he was a man! Such a thing had never happened to Lizzie before. Even her drunken admirer had not held her so tightly. 'I said . . .' she began again, her voice breathless.

'I heard you Lizzie,' he said, his voice stirring wisps of hair that the dancing had loosened about her face. 'I was trying to pretend you were enjoying this as much as I am. Stop worrying. You're doing beautifully. If you'd let yourself go, you'd be as good a dancer as your sister.'

She opened her mouth, and shut it again. She *had* been terrified of dancing, of making a fool of herself. How had he known that? And how dare he tell her he knew! A gentleman would have . . . She caught Jane's approving eye in the middle of the thought, and her face flushed. She even found herself smiling, and wondered how she could have forgotten herself so easily.

Zek Gray twirled her around and around, until her head spun and she clung to him helplessly. She didn't realise they were outside until the cool air struck her flushed, warm face, and she opened her eyes to the stars. He was still holding her, looking down at her. She thought he was going to kiss her, and waited in trepidation.

'Well?' he said, slightly breathless. His eyes laughed at her, reading her thoughts correctly.

For a moment she didn't know what he was talking about, and then it came flooding back. 'I don't . . .'

'Come Lizzie, you've no choice,' he cut in impatiently. 'You needn't see much of me, if that's what's worrying you. I'm working all day and only come in at night, and then I'm too tired to do much more than eat and sleep. Certainly too tired to break down doors and force myself upon shrinking maidens. Your so-called virtue is quite safe where I'm concerned.'

She sniffed. 'I thought no such thing! How dare you insinuate . . .'

'Lizzie,' he said, and despite the softness of it she came to a halt, looking up at him rather uncertainly. 'Well?' he asked again.

'Despite your insults, Mr Gray, I can see the good points in your offer. I need the work and the money. I agree to be your housekeeper.'

His hands were still holding her arms, and now they tightened. 'You sound as if I've just sentenced you to ten years' hard labour,' he retorted sarcastically.

She said nothing, remembering her father, and wondering what he would say if she mentioned the fact that he was a man who had been in prison. The stillness enclosed them. After a moment she felt his breath stirring her hair, but dared not look up.

'Lizzie Banister,' he whispered, 'have I ever told you you've the longest lashes of any woman of my acquaintance?'

She felt his lips on her cheek, gently caressing. Her heart had begun to beat irregularly, and her body stiffened in self-defence.

'Don't,' she said in a strangled voice.

He laughed, and nibbled at her ear, sending a series of shocking thrills over the sensitive skin. 'I'd like to meet the man who finally tames you,' he told her.

'You needn't be afraid it'll be you,' she said jerkily, and heard him catch his breath.

'If I wanted to, I could have had you on collar and lead by now,' he told her after a moment. 'Eating out of my hand, Lizzie!'

Her furious silence challenged that statement.

He tilted up her chin, and bending kissed her lightly on the lips. 'If I want something badly enough, I take it,' he said.

With a twist of her body she was free, standing facing him angrily. 'How dare you presume I would want . . . that I would . . . how dare you!'

But he laughed. 'If I wanted a mistress, I would find myself a soft, pliant kitten of a woman. Not an alley cat with claws. As it so happens I want a housekeeper, nothing more.'

'And an . . . an alley cat will do for that?' she spat.

'Oh, admirably.'

'Lizzie? Mr Gray?' Jane appeared in the doorway, looking from one to the other uncertainly. Zek Gray stepped forward with a smile.

'Jane. Or is it Mrs Duff, now?'

'Jane, Mr Gray. You know I consider you a proper friend.'

'Then Zek, please, Jane. Lizzie and I have had a little chat, and she has been kind enough to offer to help me out of difficulty. I need a housekeeper, and your sister has accepted that position.'

Jane looked at Lizzie wide-eyed. 'Lizzie, you know you don't have to go. You know that Johnny and I would only be too glad . . .'

And yet, underneath it all, did Jane not seem relieved? Lizzie came forward to take her sister's hands. 'I know, love, and I'm grateful. But . . . Mr Gray has work for me, and I am someone who needs to work. You and Johnny don't need me now. I'd only be in the way.'

'Oh Lizzie.' Jane hugged her so hard she was smothered.

Behind them Zek Gray said dryly, 'I think we should start tonight, Miss Banister. There's no point in dawdling. And besides, in a few hours it'll be daylight.'

Lizzie glared at him. 'I will collect my bag.'

Jane met his eyes when she had gone. 'You *will* look after her, Mr . . . Zek?'

'Don't you trust me, Jane?' The dark eyes mocked. 'You did, once.'

She hung her head. 'Lizzie is not like me. She's like a child, sometimes. And she speaks her mind, and can be . . . unreasonable. But she's loyal and honest and . . .'

'All things admirable, I'm sure.' He bent to kiss her cheek. 'Don't worry, I won't hit her. I promise you that, and believe me such a promise will exhaust my will-power!'

She smiled.

'And I'll remember what you said to me in confidence before,' he added in a softer voice. 'Jane, she doesn't seem—'

She flushed, opened her mouth to speak, but at that moment Johnny appeared at her side, a little the worse for drink. He kissed her on the mouth, grinning rather idiotically. Jane chuckled, and slipped away to help Lizzie pack.

Lizzie had already changed into her old brown gown, and was sitting staring at her bag.

'Liz? Are you quite sure?'

Her sister looked up, brown eyes sparkling with the light of battle. 'Sure as I can be. And don't worry, I'll show Mr Gray what a proper housekeeper is. And I'll show him, too, what a proper lady is. He'll be sorry he . . . well, he'll be sorry.'

The two girls went outside, and Johnny helped Lizzie up on to the saddle, fixing her bag in place. Zek mounted in front.

'Put your arms around me, Miss Banister,' he said silkily, and even contrived to make that simple request improper.

'Must I?'

'Unless you wish to fall off.'

She put her arms around him as though he was a sack of potatoes, her muscles rigid with disgust. He smiled down at Bess and Johnny, and touched his heels to the horse's sides, sending it galloping off on to the road. Lizzie clung on, straining back over her shoulder to see the last of the tavern and her little sister. They were swallowed up in a moment, in the darkness of the bush. She had an urge to weep.

'I beg you not to dampen my coat,' came a sarcastic voice from in front of her.

'You . . . I hate you!'

'Hardly sentiments an employee should be expressing to her employer.'

She bit her lip. 'I was worrying. About Jane and . . . Did you know Mr Duff is . . . was transported?'

There was a pause. 'I take it that fact upsets your snobbish, narrow little mind, Lizzie?'

He sounded cold, and scornful, the caressing note quite gone from his deep voice. She didn't think she liked it as well; she certainly didn't like the implied criticism.

'I just don't think it's proper, that's all!'

'And would you consider it more proper if Jane had found herself a rich merchant who was everything he should be in the eyes of the world, but who had the unfortunate habit of beating her in private and making her the most miserable girl in the colony?'

'I didn't mean that! You twist my words.'

He shrugged. 'Then make your judgments with the things that matter.'

'I was trying to!'

'Lizzie,' he said quietly, 'sometimes I find myself disliking you intensely.'

They rode on in silence. After a time the anger left her, and she became drowsy, and her head nodded, eyelids drooping. At some stage she half woke, aware that she was no longer riding pillion, but had somehow been transferred to the front and was lying across the saddle, her head turned into his chest while one strong arm supported her. But she was too tired to be outraged by this fact, and fell asleep again almost at once.

CHAPTER
FIVE

SHE woke to full daylight, blinking like a possum in a tree. 'Here,' said Zek Gray, and something soft and aromatic was placed in her hand. Bread? She took a bite of the thick slices and tasted cheese. She began to look about her with more interest.

They were in a town. One wide street and a few cottages with verandahs. A group of men by a blacksmith's open doors eyed them with the interest of people who rarely saw strangers. She cuddled closer before she realised what she was doing, and jerked away, looking at him accusingly.

An eyebrow lifted mockingly. 'You've slept like a child, Miss Banister.'

She wasn't certain if that was a compliment or otherwise. Knowing Zek Gray, she suspected it was otherwise. She cleared her throat.

'Do you think I may stretch my legs, Mr Gray?'

After a moment he nodded. They were outside the town now, and she found shelter for her bodily concerns. When she returned he was sitting on a stump, smoking something foul-smelling she rather thought was a cigar.

'There's water here,' he said, and she saw the water-bottle beside him. It tasted rather warm, but it was good.

Her limbs were stiff and cramped, and she stretched a moment, grateful for the freedom from the horse, until she caught him watching her, rather like a circus ringmaster watches one of his acts. He rose to his feet then, and remounted, holding down his hand. His fingers closed hard on hers, and he swung her up with ease, so that she sat behind him again, her arms about his waist. The horse pranced a little, evidently feeling more refreshed from the break than Lizzie. She clung tighter, feeling the thud of his heart, and the rigid control of his body as he set the animal back on the road.

Lizzie sighed. She was quite sure Cook would never have approved of this sort of thing. It was quite unladylike to ride pillion with a man of his character. But this was not England, and things were just not the same, no matter how hard she tried to pretend they were. Perhaps that was what made it so difficult to continue acting in a manner befitting a woman of good morals and principles?

His voice interrupted these cogitations.

'We have to cross the mountains before we can get to Bathurst, which is on the other side,' he said.

Looking ahead she saw them. Quite blue they were too, seemingly covered in impenetrable bush, and dauntingly alien to an eye used to seeing nature under control by man.

'It's not that they're particularly high mountains,' he went on. 'But they consist of lots of ridges and ravines, so the going can be slow and tedious, if the weather's at all bad.'

Lizzie swallowed. 'Aren't . . . aren't there bushrangers?'

His smile was sardonic, as he glanced at her pale face over his shoulder. 'You'd be a match for any bushrangers, Miss Banister.'

She stiffened up with anger, like the alley cat he'd likened her to.

After a moment he added, 'Put your hand in the

saddle-bag on the left. That's it. Now what do you feel?'

She looked at him. 'A gun!'

'Precisely,' he said, and she knew that her breathless statement had amused him. She was constantly amusing him, it seemed! Well, once they reached this farm of his and she settled in to the way of things, this journey would be but a bad dream.

She imagined how it would be, the two-storey farmhouse with roses at the door, and . . . and green fields for cows and sheep. A stream nearby, maybe, and a village a brisk walk down the road. She smiled, the fact that she was thinking in terms of an English scene not disturbing her in the least.

As the day wore on, the land grew much hillier, and the bush much denser. They climbed, twisting this way and that, past gullies and ravines, sometimes the inclines by the road were littered with half-covered rocks and boulders, precariously poised. They stopped around noon for some salted meat and more of the bread. Zek Gray started a small fire with leisurely expertise, and began to brew some tea. The silence was quite frightening, and apart from the call of birds, they might have been the only two people left in the world.

Lizzie walked into the trees a little, until she came to a mighty chasm, and stood gazing down at the sheer, crumbling rock face, studded with tall, green-grey gums. Far below, trees massed in the narrow bottom, their tops effectively screening her sight from what lay beneath. She felt her heart catch at the sight, and for the first time since her arrival in Sydney Town, Lizzie did not feel quite so distrustful of the country.

When she returned, the tea was ready, and she took it uncomplainingly, watching Zek over the wave of rising heat which the flames made in the still, hot air.

'It might make a storm if it doesn't cool down,' he said, meeting her eyes. 'Are you frightened of thunder, Miss Banister?'

'Of course not.'

'No, you wouldn't be.' He looked away, missing her glare.

She sipped the tea, shifting her boots away as a number of ants began to move purposefully towards them. The ground seemed dry, and she perched on a boulder to keep her skirts as clean as possible. The trees hovered about them, rising far into the overcast sky, their trunks smooth and white. Ghost gums, Zek Gray had called them. And there were blue gums, and iron barks. All strange to poor Lizzie.

'How long have you been in Australia, Mr Gray?'

'Almost fifteen years,' he said. 'I came out when I was not quite twenty, and I've only been on a few business trips out of the country since.' He smiled mockingly. 'Not that I have spent all that time in this part of the colony, Miss Banister. I have had rather a . . . eh, chequered career.'

She gave him a look. 'So I should imagine.'

He laughed softly. 'A man can make quite a bit of money from sheep, though the work's hard. That's what I mainly farm, Miss Banister. Sheep.'

'I see.'

He eyed her consideringly. 'Do you? I'm beginning to wonder if I do. I enjoy it, I suppose, or I wouldn't have stuck it this long, but sometimes I wonder how I'll feel in another twenty years or so. I suppose I could sell up now, and move on, but . . . I'm thirty-five, Miss Banister. I suppose I should be

thinking of settling down permanently. But somehow a wife and brats has never appealed much to
me.'

She flushed indignantly. 'Brats! You mean children, Mr Gray.'

He smiled. 'For all your righteous anger, Miss
Banister, I didn't notice you having much success
with the . . . eh, child, at your sister's wedding.'

'I'm sure,' she said maliciously, 'you'd make an
excellent father.'

He watched her a moment, black eyes narrowing. 'Why aren't *you* married, Miss Banister?'

'I . . .' her look was accusing, 'I did not have the
opportunity while I was younger, and now of
course I am too old.'

He laughed, tossing the dregs from his cup to one
side. 'Oh indeed, you're nearly four score and ten
years, I take it?'

'Hardly that.'

'No lovers? No tragic stories to tell me? No
sweethearts tragically struck down before the
banns could be called?'

She remembered the stolen kiss in the passageway, and bowed her head so that he wouldn't see
her flush.

His smile was crooked. 'I see.'

'It's not . . . that is . . . I have not . . .' But he
looked so smug she was suddenly angry, and
looked up with sparkling brown eyes. 'You, of
course, have led a blameless life, Mr Gray?'

'Well, Miss Banister, I hardly expected anything
like this from you! Can it be you're hinting you
want to hear about my amours? All of them? Have
we the time?'

'You know very well I don't wish to hear your
sordid stories.'

His smile mocked her. 'No? Another time then?'

He turned away before she could retort. She was burning with contempt and frustration, but she kept it inside, bubbling, while they rode off. She was his housekeeper. His lecherous life was nothing to do with her. If some women were willing to respond to his black, bold looks then let them make fools of themselves. Lizzie Banister had far too much good sense.

They reached Bathurst in the darkness. The thunder had been rumbling about them, and lightning showed them the way. Lizzie had dozed against his back, her arms aching, her legs cramped from the unfamiliar position. The town was revealed to her as a number of impressive-looking stone buildings and smaller houses, in a wide dusty street. It was quite a large settlement and if it hadn't been for the daggers of lightning piercing the sky she might have gazed about with more interest.

'This is the York Hotel,' Zek said, his voice startling her.

She saw the bulk of a two-storey building, and was grateful to slide down and cling to the railings while a youngish man came running to take the horse. Doors opened, lamplight shone, and somehow they were inside a modest, clean entrance hall. A woman with a big white apron came forward, smiling.

'Mr Gray!'

He spoke with her, while Lizzie leaned with exhaustion against the wall, and watched him a little dizzily. He looked tired too, and a little the worse for wear; his face was dark with stubble, his hair dusty. She herself felt gritty and dusty, and longed for nothing so much as a wash and bed.

'Miss Banister?' She looked up. The woman,

who was introduced to her as Mrs O'Driscoll, was smiling. 'Your room is this way.'

Upstairs they went, and it was not until she turned on the landing that she realised Zek Gray was still standing down in the hall. He grinned up at her, looking more than ever like a dangerous rake in his dishevelled condition.

'I have business to attend to in the morning,' he said. 'We will meet for luncheon, hmm?'

'Thank you.'

His mouth curled a little into laughter. 'My pleasure! Sleep well, Lizzie.'

Her room was small but clean, and Lizzie was glad of the privacy to wash and fall into bed. She was tireder than she had ever been before in her life, and soon fell asleep.

She woke suddenly, lying and blinking at her surroundings. The room was light, because she had forgotten to draw the curtains, and she rose, various aches and pains causing her to groan as she made her way to the window.

The room looked out to the stables and court-yard at the back of the York Hotel. It seemed quite busy, and she could hear clatter and voices from the lower storey of the building.

The water from last night had cooled, but she washed again, sponging herself all over, and dressed in her grey serge. Housekeeper material, she felt, brushing her hair and fixing it rigorously into a knot at her nape.

Breakfast was brought to her on a tray, and she ate well, feeling ravenous after her previous exertions. She wondered what business Zek Gray had to perform, but put him from her mind as swiftly as possible. She thought instead of her sister and new husband, as she descended the stairs to the hall.

Mrs O'Driscoll came, smiling good mornings. 'Mr Gray was up early,' she offered. 'Perhaps you'll see him at lunch?'

'Yes, he said something of the sort.'

She smiled warmly, and Lizzie knew Zek had taken another victim hook, line and sinker.

'Mr Gray is quite often a visitor here. I must say I look forward to seeing him—he has a way with the ladies of Bathurst, has Mr Gray. Quite a heartbreaker.'

'So I believe,' Lizzie murmured dryly.

Mrs O'Driscoll was dying to find out who or what Lizzie was, but when Lizzie didn't enlighten her she made excuses of work to be done and went away.

With a sigh of relief, Lizzie slipped outside into the street.

The sun was warm on her head, and she made her way with a leisurely tread along the building fronts, gazing about her with wide-eyed interest. There were plenty of people about, and vehicles and horses. Everything seemed in a bustle this morning. There were a lot of red-coated soldiers about, too, and she remembered hearing somewhere that Bathurst was a military post.

It seemed quite fashionable for such a provincial centre. There were lots of shops, and she spent some time gazing a little enviously at the lacy gowns and daring hats. 'Of course, they would look quite ridiculous on me,' she said briskly to herself, 'like a . . . a hedgesparrow done up as a peacock.' But her voice was a little mournful.

What had Zek Gray said? 'I can see you in blue silk, with . . . with feathers'? Yes, feathers . . . Good God, she thought with a warm blush, what a ridiculous sight that would be!

It was as if the thought of the man had conjured

him up in the flesh, for suddenly he appeared in the glass. A jaunty little gig was passing behind her, reflected quite plainly in the window, and in it were seated Zek Gray and a woman. A pretty little woman with dancing dark curls and pouting red lips. As they passed, she saw Zek Gray lean over and plant a kiss on those red, red lips.

For some reason Lizzie didn't understand her blood ran cold. As though her body had gone to ice—quite numb. And then, just as swiftly, she felt hot, and incredibly angry. Her hands clenched into fists, and it was all she could do not to turn and shout abuse at the retreating couple. The lecher! She stared blindly in at the abundant display of hats. The lying, cheating lecher! Her own flushed, angry face glared back at her, and she met the eyes and saw, beyond the rage, something almost like despair.

The thought frightened her a little, and she turned away, walking vaguely in the direction of the hotel. Mrs O'Driscoll was right. He was a heart-breaker. She regained her room, and some of her calm, before he arrived.

He was in good spirits—and she knew why!—and made polite conversation while he escorted her downstairs to the dining-room. She wasn't hungry, and hardly ate at all, picking at her food and staring glumly at the congealing gravy. He seemed to notice it at last and frowned at her over a forkful of potato.

'Sulking, Miss Banister? Or are you ill?'

Something in the mockery of his voice sounded almost like concern, but she refused to believe it.

'I'm not hungry, Mr Gray, that's all.'

He shrugged. After a moment he said, 'I've decided not to start for home until the morning, so

we will remain here overnight. Perhaps you wish to
see something of the town?'

'Thank you, no.'

He looked at her thoughtfully, some of his good
humour leaving him. 'As you wish. I have an
appointment for dinner, so I will make arrangements for yours to be served in your room, if that is
satisfactory?'

Arrangements for tonight, had he? And she
knew what they were!

'Perfectly. Now, if you will excuse me . . .' She
rose to her feet.

'Miss Banister?'

She looked down, her face expressing merely
cold inquiry.

'Do you want an advance on your wages? I'm
sure you must wish to purchase some new clothes.
Something a little less . . . intimidating perhaps?'

'I hardly think a housekeeper is in need of
fashionable finery, Mr Gray. Good afternoon.'

She strode out of the room, her back ramrod
straight. Cook would have been proud of her,
rebuffing him so.

She tried to occupy herself in the afternoon,
stitching and reading an improving work, but her
mind kept returning to the gig and the kiss she had
seen exchanged, and her powerful imagination ran
riot.

'Miss Banister?'

A tap on the door, and Lizzie rose and went to
open it. She was already dressed and packed and
ready to leave. She had been for over an hour now.
She had not slept very well, and in the end had
come to the conclusion that she was being very
foolish. She was going to be Mr Gray's house-

keeper, nothing more, and from now on must keep that in her mind at all times. If the man wished to act like a Don Juan, it was not for her to object or otherwise.

'We must retain perfect politeness at all times,' Cook had always instructed her. 'What "they" do is no concern of ours, Banister.'

'Yes, Cook.'

'We are shadows in their lives, there to serve them.'

'Yes, Cook.'

'Keep a proper distance between yourself and "them", Banister.'

The memories upheld her, and she smiled coolly at him in her best upper-servant manner. 'Mr Gray.'

He eyed her a little uncertainly. 'You're ready?'

'Thank you, yes.'

'We'll breakfast first, I think.' He eyed her again, with a hint of suspicion.

She closed the door, thinking as she did so that he was remarkably fresh-looking for one who had spent the night in debauchery. She supposed, idly, that one grew used to such things in time, and they did not affect one as they did an ordinary human being.

'What are you thinking of, Miss Banister, to make you scowl so blackly?'

She glanced up guiltily as they descended the stairs. 'I don't remember.'

One eyebrow lifted. He let his gaze drop to her grey gown. 'Perhaps you are regretting not taking up my offer of some new clothes?'

'Indeed not! What I have will do very well, thank you.'

'Oh they're respectable enough, I grant you.'

But the thought didn't seem to please him, and he sat opposite her with an air of reflection. They ate in silence. Lizzie wondered how Jane was. She missed her already. She felt suddenly lost and adrift; as if she had been cast out into an unfamiliar, hostile world. As indeed she supposed she had.

'This is the third time you've sighed so deeply, Miss Banister,' an irritated voice said. 'Perhaps you'd tell me what the matter is?'

She looked up in surprise. 'I didn't realise I had sighed. I was thinking of Jane.'

'Should that make you so glum? Your sister seemed remarkably happy with the way things turned out. She is very capable of looking after herself. She doesn't need you.'

'Thank you,' she hissed, and stood up abruptly. 'I shall wait outside.'

She stood fuming in the morning sunshine, wondering why he was always making her lose her temper. It was as if he enjoyed baiting her into rash retaliations. She bit her lips, blinking away unaccustomed tears. He was right. Jane was perfectly capable of taking care of Johnny and herself. She had shown that while Lizzie was so ill. Jane had grown and flown, and Lizzie must make her own life.

A hand rested on her shoulder, making her jump. She spun around, glaring up into Zek's handsome face. He pulled a wry expression.

'I don't need to ask what you're thinking of, grinding your teeth there. Are you ready to go?'

'Indeed I am!'

'No last minute changes of mind?' he murmured, putting her bag back in place.

Was he hoping for one? Well, he would be disappointed. She had agreed to the job and if he was beginning to think he had made a mistake in hiring so virtuous and strait-laced a lady, then that was just too bad.

'No changes of mind,' she said smugly, and put her hand in his.

He held it for a moment, looking down into her flushed face. The dark eyes teased her. 'I'm holding you to that,' he said quietly, and pulled her lightly up into the saddle behind him.

She clung to his waist, her cheeks hot, wondering what he was about now. Or was it just another of his ploys to make her colour like a fool? He kicked the horse to a gallop through the town, and she concentrated on their surroundings. They were passing a largeish establishment for drinking when a voice hailed him.

'Zek!' A woman in some sort of brief, lacy chemisette was leaning out of a top window, her bosom almost overflowing, her dark ringlets falling either side of her pretty pouting face. She waved her hand and he waved back with a grin. They were gone in an instant, but it was long enough for Lizzie to recognise the woman from the day before. She sat stiff as a poker, her silence as condemning as words, as they rode on.

'A friend of mine,' he observed, amusement warming his deep voice.

Lizzie said nothing. Far be it for her to air her views to such a rake! Besides, he was obviously past redemption.

'Is something disturbing you? I feel as if I'm riding in front of a lobster. All brittle shell and cold flesh.'

'Far be it for me to make judgments upon fellow human beings, Mr Gray,' she said sharply, and bit her lip on her rashness.

He laughed softly. 'But you are anyway. You don't even know who she is, or why she was so friendly. Hardly British justice?'

'I don't really care to find out, Mr Gray.'

'You prefer to let your imagination take over, eh? I've met your sort before. Frustrated spinsters gossiping about things they secretly wish had happened to themselves!'

'That is not so! If you choose to . . . to consort with ladies of ill-repute, that is entirely up to you.'

He shouted with laughter, and she sat in silent humiliation while he made some attempt to control himself.

'One would think a proper lady would have too much self-respect and . . . and dignity, to be seen in public in so little,' she added stingingly.

His voice was dry. 'I thought it most becoming on her.'

'Indeed.'

'Which means my taste is not worth bothering about, Miss Banister? Well . . .' he glanced at her over his shoulder, and his smile was wicked. 'I'm sure even you would look becoming in it.'

'How dare you!'

'I don't. Shall we change the subject? Tell me, what training have you had in the art of housekeeping? I assume you're experienced. Your sister told me something about a house in London.'

She bit her lip. 'I worked in a town house for eight years. I began as a 'tweeny, and moved up to parlour maid. I was even considered for the position of lady's maid, but illness forced me . . . that is, I became ill and had to leave.'

'Leave?'

'Well I . . .' Best make a clean breast of it, she thought, and continued in rather ringing tones. 'I was in the workhouse for a year after that, but it was perfectly respectable, Mr Gray, I do assure you—' She felt his back stiffen, and hurried on nervously. 'All very clean and proper. We had our own tasks and . . . and—'

'Workhouse!' his loud shout made her jump and almost topple off the horse, which also gave a nervous jerk. 'You mean to tell me they put you into the workhouse, because you were too ill to work?'

'Well, they were employing me to work, and if I could not . . . What else could they do? It's quite commonplace, Mr Gray.'

'And you agree with it, do you?' he shouted. 'By God, Lizzie Banister, I'd like to shake you! You calmly stand there and tell me that you let them put you into the workhouse—'

'I could hardly stop them, and I'm sitting, not standing.'

He glared at her over his broad shoulder. 'You've very calm about it all.'

'There was little I could do at the time,' she retorted reasonably. 'I was too ill to argue with them.'

'Ah!' he said, the anger leaving him.

He was quiet a moment, and when he spoke again his voice was so harsh she was surprised, and a little afraid.

'I would like to meet your employers on a dark night, Miss Banister. I would like to, indeed I would.' There seemed nothing to say after that, and they fell silent.

The land around Bathurst was undulating plains, quite prosperous looking. Large homesteads sprawled on higher land, watching over paddocks of sheep, wheat and corn, and orchards of budding fruit. Summer was coming closer, and the land was getting ready to yield. Lizzie looked about her with interest, for once forgetting to hold herself rigidly away from the lecher in front of her, her hands clasping his waist, her head turning first this way, and then the other.

'I've never seen anything like it,' she said at last.

'I think you echo quite a few voices when you say that, Miss Banister. It took us around thirty years to get to discovering a way over the Blue Mountains, and when we did we found land enough for nearly everyone here on the other side. Rich plains, as you see. Anyone who had sufficient courage, trekked over to find themselves a new home.'

'But was there not enough before?'

'The better land closer to Sydney Town, the tracts by the rivers, had been taken by the first settlers. The rest was mostly hard work for little return.'

There were some men working in a field close to the road they were travelling, and Lizzie watched them, brown backs bent. Another man rode a horse, cantering up and down, his big hat shading his features. He seemed to be watching them.

'Of course, none of it could have been done without convict labour,' Zek Gray added, seeing the direction of her gaze. 'The colony was founded on the backs of convicts, and though they tell me it's a penal colony most of us are beginning to think the convicts are here for our convenience, and not the purging of their souls!'

'How far is your farm, Mr Gray?'

'Not too far now, Miss Banister. We'll stop up ahead for something to drink and rest the horse, and if we make quick time we should be there by nightfall.'

Lizzie sighed. She would never get used to this talk of 'not far' and 'a few mile up the road', when things were so painfully obviously hours away. What she had thought of in England as quite distant they considered no more than a good day's drive here.

They stopped soon afterwards for their lunch. A small tavern with a cool, dim interior played host to them. Zek ordered a tankard of ale, and drank it with a sigh. He caught her eyes over the brim and grinned.

'Do you want one, Miss Banister?'

'Thank you, no. Water will be quite sufficient.'

He shrugged. 'I've bespoken the back room for you, if you want to wash and tidy up a bit. You look rather tired.'

'Thank you.' His kindness threw her off balance, and she flushed yet again.

He put his hand out and lifted her chin, to the amused interest of the other occupants of the tap-room. 'You look peaky, Lizzie. Are you sure you feel all right?'

'Of course. I . . . I'm stronger than I look, Mr Gray.'

He scanned her face a moment more, and then dropped her chin with another shrug, as though he'd suddenly lost interest. She hurried to the back room to tidy herself, and cool her burning cheeks with cold water. What on earth was wrong with her? She must try and preserve a little dignity. She took several deep breaths, and turning caught the laughing eye of a young woman with dark hair and a dusty, well-darned gown.

'Sorry, did I startle you? I was just after asking if you had all you needed. Your husband told me to make you comfortable.'

'Oh, I . . . that is . . .'

'There's a bed there. Well, near enough to a bed, and you can rest up for an hour or two, he says, until it's cooler outside. No sense riding out in the full heat of the sun, is there?'

'He's not my husband,' Lizzie managed, sitting down on the bench.

The girl's eyebrows rose a little. 'Well, it don't matter to me if you're married or not.'

'I don't mean . . . oh dear.'

But the girl was smiling and her eyes were friendly.

'I'm to be Mr Gray's housekeeper.'

The smile broadened. 'Ah! I'm a housekeeper myself. Of a sort, that is. I used to be a scullery maid, in England, but since then I've been lots o' things.'

'Are you a bounty girl too?' Lizzie whispered.

The girl pulled a wry face. 'Not likely. I was sent out, thieving see. I spent a time in Sydneyton, working in a house there, then I come out to Bathurst to help in a confectionery shop the master was startin' up, but it didn't work out, so I ended up out here.'

Another felon! Good God, how did one treat them? She shuffled a moment, smoothing her skirts. 'I suppose . . . I suppose you meet lots of travellers here?'

'Quite a few, aye.' The girl frowned. 'Did you say you was to be housekeeper for Mr *Gray*? Not Zek Gray, is it? I heard o' him, you see. Is he still wearing the willow for that Angelica Bailey, or is it t'other way round?'

'I don't know. That is . . .' Lizzie's eyes had widened.

The girl moved closer. 'Didn't you know any-

thing about it then? I had her in here one day. Like
a duchess she was, sweeping around the tap-room,
finding fault with all. Oh she's beautiful all right,
but . . .' she pulled a face. 'Still, it ain't your
business, is it?'

'No, it isn't . . . ain't . . . I mean, *isn't*.' She
smiled firmly. 'I really am rather tired. I think I will
sleep for a moment.'

The girl nodded. 'I'll leave you then.'

'No doubt Mr Gray will tell me when he wants to
leave.'

An eyebrow rose. 'So that's Mr Gray,' the
girl muttered, 'I thought it were just one o' his
workers.' She grinned. 'That explains everythin''
then, don't it? I mean, you'd expect women to go
mad for a man like that, wouldn't you?'

Lizzie lay fuming when she had gone. Women to
go mad indeed! For what? A handsome, knowing
smile and a bold, bad eye? And who was Angelica
Bailey? The little brunette with the red lips in
Bathurst? No, she had been pretty certainly, but
not exactly beautiful. Angelica Bailey was obviously an experience yet to come!

CHAPTER
SIX

THEY reached the homestead at evening.

It was flatter country here, apart from one slope, and on this was set a low, sprawling building surrounded with sheds and various barns and cottages, all black against a sunset of orange and gold and crimson. A number of trees towered on the far side. Lizzie was tired, but still managed to stir some response to the beauty of it all.

'Is this all yours?' she asked faintly.

He laughed. 'Afraid so.'

'You said a farm!' she cried accusingly. The image of the English farmhouse faded. It was frightening, seeing this great spread. Lizzie felt uneasy and rather lost at the very thought of it all.

'It's called Primrose Hill, but when I took over it seemed to become merely *Gray's*.'

'Gray's,' she murmured.

As they drew closer woodsmoke stung her nostrils, and she could see a light, and people, approaching. A voice rang out, and suddenly a man appeared at their side. Zek Gray drew his mount to a halt.

'Mr Gray!'

'Ralph. Hold Star.' The man held the bridle, and Zek slid down. Lizzie's face shone out white and uncertain. Ralph frowned up at her. 'Mr Gray . . . ?'

'Wait on man. Lizzie!' he held up his arms and

caught her waist as she slid down. Her legs
wavered, and she clung to him for a moment, giving
Ralph a pretty picture and much to ponder on, as
Zek Gray held her close. He eyed his boss with
interest.

'Are you all right?' Gray demanded quite
sharply.

'Yes. Just a little stiff, thank you.' She stood
away, smoothing her skirts and trying to ignore the
interested eyes. Zek retrieved her bag.

'This way.'

There were other people about, but beyond a
wave and a smile, he ignored them, and led Lizzie
on towards the big house. There was a verandah
surrounding two sides of it, and the windows were
shuttered, though lamplight shone out through the
slats. Lizzie shivered. How many servants would he
have to run it? That would mean giving orders and
. . . At that moment the door was flung open, and
she held up a hand to shield her eyes from the
sudden glare penetrating the darkness.

'Mr Gray?'

A feminine voice, low and competent. Lizzie saw
an opulent figure outlined against the light, and
smelled lavender and sweat.

'Jessie,' Gray murmured. His hand tightened on
Lizzie's arm and dragged her unceremoniously forward. The room was cool, and sparsely furnished,
but she hardly noticed that. 'This is Miss Banister,
Jessie, who will be taking over the position of
housekeeper. Lizzie, this is Jessie Grant, Ralph's
wife. She is the cook, but has kindly given her spare
time to ordering my staff until I finally got around
to hiring someone like you.'

There was a stillness, and even though she was so
tired and bewildered, Lizzie knew the other woman

was upset. So, she was taking the other's place? He didn't really need a housekeeper at all!

'How do you do Miss Banister,' Jessie Grant said quietly, the greeting cool and polite.

They shook hands, and Lizzie tried to smile.

'Come into the sitting-room, Miss Banister, and I'll find you some tea. Mr Gray, you must be hungry?'

'A bit, Jessie, a bit. Perhaps you could show Lizzie the ropes in the morning? She's worn out tonight.' His smile was almost tender, confusing Lizzie even further, and Jessie eyed her balefully.

'Of course, sir.'

The sitting-room was small; tidy and cosy—chairs, a sofa, a sideboard and some shelves. A desk in one corner was strewn with papers, and there was a stone fireplace, a small fire making the room seem even cosier. Lizzie had not realised until then how the temperature outside had dropped, and she came close to the flames, warming her hands. Her eyes travelled back to the other woman.

Buxom, as she'd first thought, with a round, dimpled face and smallish blue eyes. Red curls tied back, clashing a little with the pink gown. She was in her thirties, and a hard life had left deeper lines on her face than perhaps would otherwise be there. She smiled at Lizzie, but something in it made her think of steel.

'I'll see about some food and the tea,' she said, turning to Gray. 'Mary can bring it in. I'd best get home to Ralph.'

'Of course. And thank you, Jessie.'

Her eyes dropped away. Lizzie was suddenly struck with the thought that it was going to be more than taking over a position of importance Jessie would resent about Lizzie. It was Zek Gray himself.

The door closed softly. Lizzie cleared her throat. 'She didn't tell me where my room was.'

'I'll show you when we've eaten.'

'Really, I'm not hungry. Just tea. I can have that in there, can't I?' She wanted to get away from him, be by herself, think.

He looked at her, noting her pallor and the dark-circled eyes. 'Very well. I'll show you and Mary can bring your tea later.'

He held open the door for her to pass through, and she went by, flicking him a glance. Narrowed eyes scanned her in a frowning face. Had she displeased him already?

Her bedroom was at the back of the house, giving out on to a corridor. 'Through here,' he said, and nodded her in.

She was out again in a moment, cheeks flushed, brown eyes glittering. 'You can't expect . . .' she stammered. 'I . . . really!'

He was laughing, his shoulders shaking, his white teeth gleaming. 'Ah God, Lizzie, you should see your face.'

'Trust you to have a bed like that,' she delivered tartly.

'But of course, I'd need a brass king-sized bed, wouldn't I? No, I'm sorry to disappoint you, Miss Banister, but the bed was there when I bought the place. The last occupant had it dragged up here to please his new wife. When they left the bed stayed. Perhaps they were already disillusioned with marriage, or perhaps they just couldn't afford to take it with them.' He shrugged.

Lizzie looked back into the room. The bed really was huge! It took up most of the room, though a few other pieces of furniture had been squeezed into the corners. One window graced the wall, and this was shuttered firmly. Someone had put a lighted lamp on the shelf near the door. The bed was covered in a patchwork counterpane which some-one—Jessie?—had turned back invitingly, and the big white pillows were fluffed up. The brasswork gleamed with loving polishing, and Lizzie wondered if that too was Jessie's work. A thought occurred to her, and she looked at him suddenly, where he stood, watching her with unreadable eyes.

'Where do you sleep, Mr Gray?'

For a moment he seemed to hesitate, and then he said, 'Just down the passageway, Miss Banister. Why? Are you offering to share with me?'

She slammed the door, and stood alone in the bedroom, his soft laughter mocking her through the wooden panels. His footsteps faded at last, and with a sigh, she began to unpack her bag. Undressing, she pulled on her familiar woollen nightgown. She unbound her hair, brushing it out in thick, luxuriant waves over her shoulders.

Lizzie eyed the bed rather suspiciously, as though afraid it might suddenly rear up at her. She sat down carefully on the mattress and sank in. It was *very* soft. She had never had anything quite like it in all her twenty-five years. Hesitantly, she slid beneath the covers, sitting up against the pillows. She felt like a child in its vast bulk, her body hardly making any impression at all under that wide expanse of coverlet.

It was the bed of a princess! She was almost frightened of it; excited too, like a little girl with a Christmas present. Why had he given her this room? She had expected some little cell with a bench-bed and maybe a dresser with a square of mirror to brush her hair in front of. That's what servants were quartered in. Not something like this. Perhaps he still had designs on her virtue? She frowned, mulling over the problem. It seemed unlikely. Lizzie was hardly a vain girl, and she could see that Zek Gray had his pick of any one of a dozen women. He would hardly choose a plain stick of a girl with a sharp tongue and an irritating habit of blushing and hair like wire.

A knock on the door startled her, and she pulled the counterpane up to her chin, her eyes big and dark in her tired face. Mary? It must be.

'Come in.'

The door opened.

He had taken off his coat, and his shirt was unbuttoned at the throat. His hair was messed too, as though he had run his hand through it. His eyes gleamed like oil in the lamplight. He was a sight to make any girl's heart flutter, and Lizzie despite everything was only a girl.

For a moment he said nothing, looking at her in the midst of the huge bed, her black hair falling about her, framing her pale, pointed face and the large brown eyes.

'You look like you've seen a ghost,' he said softly, his voice husky and strange.

'Or a wolf,' she managed, but her tone lacked its usual sting.

He smiled briefly. 'I forgot to tell you that I expect you to present yourself at eight tomorrow morning in my office. I can start you off officially then, as my housekeeper. All right?'

'Oh. Thank you.'

'And I've informed Mary she's to bring you a tray in here.'

'Thank you, sir.'

Why did he stare so? Hadn't he ever seen a woman in bed? The thought made her blush, and she longed for Cook's tart comments on what to do in such a situation. He was being so kind to her, how could she order him out?

'Comfortable?' he asked at last, smiling.

'Very, thank you.' She sounded shy—why did his warm look make her so stupid? At least when he made her angry she could retaliate.

'Better than the workhouse sleeping accommodation, eh?'

She wondered, suddenly, if that was why he had given her the room with this ridiculous bed in it. Because he was being kind and . . . no, the idea was quite out of character! He must have some ulterior motive.

He was still watching her. She lifted her chin and met his gaze suspiciously. The mocking smile he gave her didn't help, and she breathed deeply.

'Much better than the workhouse, Mr Gray. Now, I am very tired and—'

She felt it then, crawling along her foot. She had screamed before she knew it, for Lizzie, like most other women, had a horror of all crawly things, and most especially spiders. Zek Gray was beside her before she could scream again.

'What is it? Lizzie?'

She squirmed beneath the covers, and when he put out his hands clutched them. 'Spider! Oh!' and she scuttled away from whatever was crawling on her under the covers. He hesitated, and then suddenly making a decision, jerked back the covers.

A long legged spider, a little drunk from the darkness and warmth of the big bed, weaved across the white sheets. He swept it off the bed, stunning it against the wall. Lizzie watched him, crouched on the further side of the mattress, as he disappeared on to the floor. There was a series of thuds, and then he swore as he hit his head on the underpart of the bed. His face appeared over the side, rather flushed, hair falling forward into his eyes.

They stared at each other a moment, and then Lizzie felt her face beginning to falter. The laughter came rattling up inside her, her eyes wept helpless tears. He too had begun to laugh, leaning weakly against the bed. She was still laughing when she felt his hand on her arm. She looked up, smiling, and found him watching her, his face still flushed with humour, and something more that she at first failed to recognise.

'Lizzie,' he murmured, and the bed went down as he stretched out beside her, pushing her back against those ridiculous pillows.

His mouth was warm and gentle, and he coaxed her lips, his hands pinioning hers either side of her face. She stiffened with surprise, and then, as he lowered his body across her, the warmth of his chest stifling her breath, she went limp. His mouth intensified its work, and he groaned with something between pleasure and pain.

She found her hands free now, for he was cupping her face. They slid quite of their own accord about his back, and she felt his muscles rippling beneath the thin stuff of his shirt. His hands were tangling in her hair. He was kissing her throat now, and somehow her nightgown had slipped off her shoulder and he was pulling it down over both shoulders, then her arms.

'No,' she said, but he ignored her.

He half rose, looking down at her bare breasts. She met his eyes, dizzy and weak though she was.

They were full of desire, and something dark and warm she couldn't analyse. She felt suddenly humble before him.

'Lizzie,' he whispered, and pressed his mouth to the valley between her breasts, 'You're lovely.'

Lovely? The word taunted her, and she closed her eyes. He would say that, of course. He knew just how to overcome her pride and fear and reserve. He would know how she craved to be beautiful. And what woman could not be flattered at being called 'lovely' by a connoisseur such as he? She pressed his face to her, feeling the heat of his flesh against hers. Everything ceased to matter then, but the need in her to be totally his.

He was taking off his shirt, and his bare chest shone brown in the lamplight. She found herself running her hands up to his shoulders, tentative, wondering, afraid any moment of rejection. He smiled, bending to nibble at her bruised lips. His hand touched her thigh, caressing, gentle as a moth's wing.

'Your legs are the longest I've ever seen,' he teased, between kisses. 'You're like a filly. A wild, shy, unbroken filly. Oh Lizzie, let me break you . . .'

His voice was muzzy, throbbing with what she herself was feeling. She tried to tell herself that last night he had been with the brunette with the red lips, and she had heard today that he loved Angelica Bailey, and even Jessie seemed to be in some way involved with him. He was a lecher, a rake, a . . . Oh, she wanted him to go on kissing and touching her forever, and telling her all those sweet, lying things he was telling her.

She opened her eyes, turning to kiss his cheek while he was nibbling her shoulder. Her eyes went beyond him, to the door where it stood ajar. A girl's shocked, white face. The rattle of a tea tray. The sight of it stunned her so that for a moment she couldn't speak. The girl, with great sang-froid, carefully set the tray on the dresser and ran.

Zek didn't seem to have heard. Lizzie felt her flesh creep with the thought of what she had just been about to do. Self-disgust and fright combined with a rushing return of her own natural prudery. Any desire she had felt was swamped, and she began to struggle, pushing at his shoulders, and finally pummelling his bare back with her clenched fists.

The fact of her unwillingness seemed to penetrate at last, and he lifted himself up on his hands, looking down into her face with black, blurred eyes. He was so devilishly handsome that for a moment she was almost lost again, but then all his perfidies came back to remind her. Lizzie rolled away from under him, dragging her nightgown up to her neck, and fumbling to button it with fingers that shook and trembled.

'No,' she said, her voice shaking and squeaky. 'No, no, no. If you . . . if you think I'm here for your convenience, Mr Gray, you may think again! I've come as housekeeper, and not as . . . as your mistress!'

He stared at her, and then pushed himself up to his knees, running his hands through his hair. His eyes slowly lost their look of confusion, and he began to pull on his shirt.

'I never suggested such a thing.'

His voice was cool and mocking. It was the last straw. He might at least tell her he loved her, that he could no longer control his feelings, that he had lost his heart to her, that . . . Why was life never like penny novels?

'Get out, Mr Gray!' she whispered, her voice shaking, and pointed at the door as she had once seen the heroine in a play do, and which had pleased the audience inordinately.

He tried to catch her, but she scuttled away to the very edge of the bed, eyes wild through her tangled hair.

'Lizzie,' he said gently, coaxingly. 'What does it matter? So much fuss. I thought you wanted me to kiss you and . . .'

'Wanted!' she cried, and fury blinded her. 'Get out, you lecher! I'm a decent woman, and that's something you obviously know nothing about. Now get out!' She picked up the pillow and flung it at him as hard as she could.

He was at the door, looking cross and rumpled. His eyes gleamed with tiredness and mockery and irritation. 'Oh I'll get out,' he said softly. 'There are plenty of others who'll welcome me to their beds, Lizzie, if you're too prudish to do so.'

'I don't care what you do,' she whispered, as he slammed the door. 'I don't care!' she repeated, and wiped the tears that were running down her flushed cheeks.

He was a monster. Like one of those men whom one read of in the newspapers, assaulting innocent women, forcing their . . . their attentions on them. She had never known exactly what 'attentions' were, until this moment. And he hadn't even had to force her! He'd used some practised, subtle trickery, some sort of magic to make her respond. She sniffed, and pushed back her hair. He must be a monster, to be able to fascinate her into such compliance! She hoped he found someone else, someone whose husband or father would give him a punch on the nose. She hoped . . .

Her tears ran out of control, and she began to sob against the pillows. The thing was, she had enjoyed it. Enjoyed the touch of his hands and lips, the breath against her flesh, the murmured endearments she had never thought to hear from such as him. It had flattered her and made her respond to him. He must have known how starved she was for compliments and affection and played on it. Cruel!

And to further complicate matters, Mary had seen her, and him, in a situation that needed no further explanation. She knew too much about servants' gossip herself to hope the girl would stay quiet. By tomorrow morning at eight, when she presented herself in that . . . that lecher's office, everyone would know. Jessie Grant and Mary and Ralph and all the other nameless faces she was yet to meet! And she would be expected to exert some control over them! She took a shaking breath, and lay still, staring at the tea tray. After a moment she rose and went over to it, pouring herself a strong cup with plenty of sugar. It was done now, and she must make the best of it. She would deny all knowledge, that was the best way. Pretend it had never happened. Eventually they must forget, although . . . and she sighed. There was probably very little to gossip about out here, and Mary's story could become a wonder for miles around.

Lizzie woke to find the place abustle with life. She lay for a moment, letting herself revel in the luxury of the big bed, until memories sent her squirming out. The curtains on her window were drawn back from open shutters, a vista over the country back towards Bathurst was revealed, and she viewed it somewhat uncertainly.

A tap on the door heralded Mary with warm water, towels and soap, which she set down on the wash-stand. The girl glanced at her slyly, but smiled a good morning. Lizzie thanked her, and washed thoroughly. She could still smell that lecher's scent on her flesh, and she scrubbed until she shone pink. Then she dressed in her clean brown gaberdine, and brushed her hair, tying it back severely.

Satisfied, she regarded herself in the mirror. She looked like a housekeeper, anyway. No one could find fault in her appearance . . . And, gazing a little sternly into her reflection, she decided no one would believe Mary's story anyway. Who would think this drab, plain creature could captivate a man like Zek Gray? It was just ridiculous, and anyone with any sense could see that at a glance.

She found the office at the front of the house, with Mary's help, and tapped on the door as if nothing were making her heart bump and her legs shake. A voice asked briskly for her to enter.

He was sitting at a desk, glancing through some letters. He looked up at her with a half-smile, polite but nothing more. She stood before him, very stiff and straight, hands clasped properly before her. Her voice was as cool as she wanted it.

'Mr Gray.'

'Miss Banister. I've asked Jessie to show you over the house and tell you what's what. She should be here shortly. Perhaps you could sit down?'

'I'd rather stand.'

'As you wish.' The matter was obviously one of indifference to him. He read through another letter, and then set it aside, straightening the pile.

'Is there any particular thing you wish me to

remember, sir? Any particular . . . instructions for me?'

He looked up, almost startled. 'Particular things?'

'Well . . . about the meals or . . . anything. Any . . . well, special fancy of yours that . . .'

He looked back at his fingers, interlocked on the desk in front of him, and she had the sudden impression he was struggling to keep in laughter.

'Eh, no, nothing like that. Ah, here's Jessie!'

There was relief in his face as Jessie Grant entered the room, and Lizzie wondered if he was glad to be rid of her, as she turned with a stiff smile of welcome.

She knew at once that Jessie knew; saw the knowledge in the other woman's blue eyes as they slid from Zek Gray to her. Lizzie wanted to shuffle her feet but dared not give way to any emotion at all.

'Mr Gray, did you rest well, sir?' There was a taunt there, but if he heard it he pretended otherwise.

'Yes, yes. Jessie, please show Miss Banister around and . . . well, inform her of anything you feel she will need to know. Is Ralph ready?'

'Yes, sir. He's around at the stables with the horses. Mrs Bailey called in while you were away, sir. She seemed most . . . eager to see you, sir.'

Lizzie wondered how he could put up with Jessie's insidious comments without slapping her plump face.

But Zek Gray seemed merely thoughtful. 'Angelica?' he frowned, and then smiled rather ruefully. 'All right. I'll ride out there later today. Thank you for telling me, Jessie. Good morning, Miss Banister.'

'Good morning, sir,' she said in a freezing voice. They went out and closed the door.

Jessie began to take her through the house, naming each room in a colourless, though very efficient manner. It was quite a large homestead, the rooms tending to lead off each other rather than on to a hallway. This was the way they had been built in the early days, Jessie Grant informed her. The furnishings were comfortable if not precisely grand, though a couple of particularly elegant pieces caught Lizzie's eye.

'Of course,' Jessie said, 'when Mr Gray marries he will wish to make the place more fitting for his wife. At the moment, however, it suits him as it stands.'

Lizzie, who had noted the fading paintwork and rather scratched wooden floors merely nodded. If Jessie was hoping for a bite she would be disappointed.

The kitchen was built a little way from the main house, in case of fire. It was hot inside, and a number of the girls were introduced to her, their eyes bold and assessing. Lizzie felt tired already with the strain of putting on a front, and wondered how she would get through the rest of the day.

'This is Ellen and Dulcie and Betty,' Jessie introduced them. 'I usually do the cooking, Miss Banister. Perhaps we could discuss menus later? I thought . . . but perhaps you will be busy tonight?'

One of the girls sniggered, and Lizzie felt her flesh go cold and numb. After a moment she said, 'Thank you, Mrs Grant, but later will suit me perfectly.'

Jessie smiled, but her eyes were gleaming with malice. 'We usually have our largest meal in the evening, with a light luncheon. Mr Gray rarely comes in to eat in the middle of the day. He has a large breakfast, and that seems to be enough for him.'

'I see.'

There was a vegetable garden and an orchard, and a few flowers at the front of the house which needed some care. The paddocks stretched away in all directions, neatly fenced. Lizzie saw men riding horses, sheep were bleating, and wheat waving. She blinked at the prospect, shading her eyes against the increasing glare of the sun.

'The Baileys' homestead is over there,' Jessie murmured close to her ear.

She looked but could not see it.

'They are our nearest neighbours, of course. Then there are the Tuckers, but they rarely visit. Mr Gray finds little in common with them.'

Lizzie looked at her in surprise. 'Why not?'

'Well . . .' Jessie smoothed her skirts. 'Mr Gray is hardly a family man, is he, Miss Banister?'

Lizzie met her eyes. They were shining, not at all friendly or kind. Jessie hated her because she thought her Zek's mistress. She hoped Lizzie got hurt. Why? Because Lizzie had taken her place? Or because Jessie was jealous of the position she imagined Lizzie held in his affections?

'Thank you, Mrs Grant,' she said suddenly. I think that is all I need to know. I shall learn, I expect, as I go along. I will go now and arrange to have the house thoroughly cleaned. I noticed quite a few areas this morning which had not been attended to in a very long time.'

Jessie's face flushed red at the criticism, but she said nothing as Lizzie turned away. Lizzie allowed herself a small smile as she made her way back to the house. Well, that should please them! They could tear her character to shreds now, knowing she loathed them just as much as they seemed to loathe her.

Somehow the day passed. She had intended to take her own meal in her room that evening, but Jessie seemed so surprised and gleeful she decided after all to eat with Zek Gray, no matter how much it cost her.

It was getting dark when he came in. Lizzie had been working herself up to this moment, and had taken special pains with her appearance, dragging her hair back and buttoning her gown up to its topmost button. She couldn't have looked plainer or more dowdy than she did at that moment, and felt rather pleased with herself.

She did not look up at the door of the sitting-room when it opened, and pretended not to hear his boots crossing the floor towards her.

'Miss Banister!' he greeted her heartily, and began to pour himself out a drink.

He had been away all afternoon at the Baileys' place. She eyed him under her lashes, seeing the pale tense look about his mouth and wondering if he really were as much in love with the beautiful Angelica as the tavern girl had hinted. Other than that, he looked tired and dusty, and seemed in genuine need of the drink.

He turned and looked at her, where she sat observing him, the glass in his hand. His eyes were quite unreadable, his smile a mere polite mask.

'How did your day go, Miss Banister? Everything satisfactory?'

'Thank you, yes.'

'Jessie show you everything you need to know?'

'Yes.' Jessie had shown her, at least, who her friends were!

'Well then . . .' he set down the now empty glass. 'I'll go and wash before dinner.'

For some reason, as they sat at the table and Mary served the meal, Lizzie kept remembering how he had held her and kissed her, the feel of his flesh under her hands, the warm smooth skin of his broad back and shoulders. Her hands shook so that she had to clench them under the table, knowing she was a fool.

He had changed his shirt, and his hair was still a little damp where the water had splashed. He seemed as preoccupied as she, staring at his plate, and eating as if it were an afterthought. There was a long, tense silence.

Lizzie drew a breath. 'I was wondering, sir, if you would allow me to work in your front garden. It seems in sad repair.'

He looked up, as though startled to see her sitting there. As if he had forgotten her existence. After a moment he bent back to his plate.

'Of course, do as you wish.'

'You're too kind.'

He looked up again, narrowing his eyes at her acidity. 'I'm rarely kind, Miss Banister, and you should remember that. By the way, I am to tell you that Mrs Bailey is calling some time to see you. She seems to think a new housekeeper merits a personal viewing, so you must prepare yourself for the ordeal.'

Lizzie's eyes grew larger. 'Ordeal? Is she so frightening then?'

He laughed sharply. 'She is . . . unusual, Miss Banister. But you must judge for yourself. By the way, I meant to tell you that if you wish any mail sent back to your sister you must have it out on the office table by Monday. All the mail goes then.'

'Thank you, Mr Gray. I'll remember.'

He drank from his glass, gazing through her. Lizzie dropped her chin, staring moodily at the table in front of her, her fingers twisting together in her lap.

'Lizzie,' he said, and then, when she looked up, bit his lip and shook his head. 'No matter,' he said softly, mockingly, and his eyes teased her lips and the high-buttoned collar of her gown and the ugly style of her hair. As if none of it existed, as if he could see her quite plainly as she had been in his arms.

After a moment she knew she couldn't sit there and let him break down all her carefully prepared defences, and she rose, excusing herself.

'Running away, Lizzie,' he said softly, but other than that let her go.

Her room was a haven, and she stood there, viewing it with a sort of relief.

The first day had come and gone, and she had survived it.

CHAPTER
SEVEN

LIFE went on. There seemed plenty to do, and Lizzie could always invent more. She spent some time in the garden, tidying it up, and planting out some bulbs she had found in the still room. Jessie Grant said they would die, because it was too late in the spring to plant, but Lizzie said nothing. The other woman was always jabbing her with little comments and innuendos. It was better to ignore them and hope, in time, she would grow tired of the game and stop it.

In fact there was plenty to be busy with, and Lizzie began to wonder how she could feel so alone in a place that buzzed with life and people. And yet she did feel alone. Zek Gray was always out, and when she saw him at meals he spoke very little more than polite pleasantries. His lips spoke them, at least, even while his black eyes teased her for her proper manner and proper clothing and proper conversation. He put a strain on her defences that she had never had to endure before.

If he had touched her, it couldn't have been worse. She almost wished he would approach her in the passageway to her bedroom, like that long ago rake had done, and then she could slap his face and make it plain she wanted none of him. But just to look . . . what could she say to him? Don't look! He would lift his eyebrows in mock amazement, or throw back his dark head and roar with laughter. And that she couldn't bear.

Angelica Bailey had called as promised. Lizzie had known who she was the moment the other woman came riding up to the homestead on a dark, spirited little mare. Other women would drive gigs, or even have someone drive them in a carriage, if they could afford it. Not Angelica. Lizzie watched her flying up the path, blonde hair tossing under a dark blue bonnet, her riding habit fitting like a glove. She was the sort of woman you expected to be the mistress of the king, or a foreign princess at least. Something special and exciting. She had restless, slanting blue eyes, and a smiling pink mouth, and her voice was quick and impatient. But she was beautiful, and Lizzie decided she was just the sort of partner Zek Gray would look for.

'Miss Banister? You are not at all plain! I shall have to berate Zek for telling me such lies, shan't I? Do you really intimidate him as much as he says you do? I do not believe he quakes in his boots, of course, but . . .'

Lizzie's rigid poise slipped a little. Her dark eyes sparkled, but all she said was, 'Tea, Mrs Bailey?'

'Please!' The woman stripped off her gloves and sat down, untying the ribbons of her bonnet, and eyeing Lizzie as she too disposed herself, on a chair by the window. 'Have you put old Grant's nose out of joint? I suppose you have, taking over like that. Just like Zek though to hire himself a watch-dog! I beg pardon, Miss Banister. But he was rather worried, poor dear, that Jessie had begun to have designs on him. It seemed a sensible way to put them to an end, without hurting Ralph.'

Lizzie blinked. 'Do you mean he . . . and you knew he was bringing me back? I was under the impression—'

That it had been a sudden decision, Lizzie had meant to ask. Zek Gray had struck her as a thoughtful man, but one who made his decisions quickly. The idea that he and Angelica had sat down and planned everything to the last detail made her very angry.

'Oh Zek tells me everything!' the woman said airily, and smiled.

She had white teeth—sharp little incisors. Like a cat, Lizzie thought, and decided the eyes were rather feline too. Glowing and watchful above the smiling pink mouth. Angelica was certainly not a name she would put to Mrs Bailey!

'Is your husband also a . . . a farmer, Mrs Bailey?'

'Squatter is the word, Miss Banister, usually applied to the men who own these large areas of land. And yes, he is. Or was. My husband is an invalid, Miss Banister, and quite old.'

Lizzie felt she understood perfectly. Mr Bailey had a beautiful wife and was unable to keep her. Angelica could do as she pleased. The tea came, and Mary set it down carefully on the table between them, bobbing a curtsey for Angelica.

'Mr Gray is coming in shortly, ma'am. I've put by an extra cup for 'im.'

Lizzie smiled, and began to pour.

'How did you meet Zek?' Angelica asked, taking her cup.

'I thought he would be sure to tell you that too,' Lizzie murmured. 'We met on the ship to Sydney Town.'

'Ah!'

But the blue eyes were hard, and curious. Lizzie knew instinctively that someone had already told her about the first night in residence, and wished once again that it had never happened.

'Zek is an attractive man, Miss Banister. He finds women a challenge, let us say. But it means nothing. He soon tires.'

Lizzie looked politely interested, though her cheeks were pink.

Angelica smiled again, leaning forward confidingly. 'Actually, I sometimes feel he's just biding time. Waiting for Mr Bailey to . . . well, you know. He's always so very attentive to me, dear Zek.'

'But how morbid,' Lizzie retorted.

Angelica's cup rattled, and she opened her mouth to retort.

'May I come in?'

They both looked up guiltily. Zek strode in, smiling first at Angelica, and then at Lizzie. The former rose with a laugh, catching his hands in hers, and tiptoed to kiss his brown cheek.

'Zek, my dear, I didn't hear you. Miss Banister has been telling me you met on board ship. How romantic!'

'Has she indeed,' he said.

He sat down beside Angelica on the sofa and watched as Lizzie poured him out some tea. Her hand shook as she held out the cup to him, but he took it without noticeable expression. Angelica's hands seemed to be all over him as she chattered about this and that, restless and possessive. Touching his shoulder, now his arm, brushing his lapel. Once she even rested her long fingers on his thigh, gazing into his eyes with a faint, feline smile. That they were lovers was plain enough without Angelica's pains to make it so blatantly obvious. Lizzie wondered if Angelica was reacting to the gossip concerning her, but thought it would hardly matter to a woman as beautiful as she.

Zek was watching Angelica, his eyes warm, but he made no move to respond to her touch, or to touch her back. He seemed content to sit back and let her do all the running. Lizzie thought him despicable, a monster who seduced old men's wives. And an invalid to boot!

At that moment Gray met her gaze over his cup, black eyes laughing with the old wickedness. Lizzie felt the colour rise into her cheeks as she realised he had read her thought. Angelica, seeing the look pass between them, seemed to take it for something entirely different, and rose to her feet almost clumsily, saying in a sharp, shrill voice:

'Well, all very cosy, but I really must go! Poor Thomas will be waiting. Goodbye, my dear.' She kissed him hard on the lips. 'Miss Banister,' a cold nod, and she turned. She looked over her shoulder to Zek at the door. 'Aren't you coming to see me off?'

'But of course, Angel.'

The sweetened form of her name made her eyes shine triumph at Lizzie, as she passed over the threshold.

Alone, Lizzie set the cups back on the tray neatly, and brushed up some spilt sugar. She went to the window, turning her back to the room, and watched until Angelica rode past. The girl was kicking her mare into a gallop, and shot headlong down the driveway towards the road, hair and skirts flying.

'Well, what do you think of her?'

She managed not to start, and answered calmly enough. 'She's very beautiful, Mr Gray.'

'Isn't she?'

He sounded harsh, and she wondered why. Angelica plainly loved him, and if he was patient he could have her for his wife as well as his lover. The fact of that hurt her, sinking into her midriff like the sudden jab of a fist. She wanted to double up with the pain, and blinked away sudden tears of she knew not what. Jealousy, perhaps, that a woman could be so beautiful.

'She has rather a sharp tongue,' he went on, 'but altogether she is pleasing to both eye and ear, is she not, Lizzie?'

She wondered why he was going on and on about it.

'She would make you a fine partner, Mr Gray. Is that what you want me to say?'

He looked tense, but soon relaxed back into mockery. He laughed at the sight of her angry white face. 'Maybe it is. She seems eager enough to accept the post. More eager than you were to accept that of housekeeper, eh, Lizzie?'

'Hardly the same, is it, Mr Gray?'

'I disagree!' He moved restlessly. 'Both positions require a certain interest in my comfort. And let me tell you, Lizzie, sometimes you make me damned uncomfortable!'

'I'm sorry.' But she wasn't, and didn't sound it.

'Oh you're most efficient, and very polite. But I get the impression, my dear Lizzie Banister, that you hate the sight of me. Perhaps you even begin to wish yourself back in the workhouse, eh? Is that it?'

'Of course not!'

She put a hand to her head, shaking it and feeling suddenly weary. What did he want? Why was he treating her so? He admitted she did her job well, what more could he ask?

Before she had realised what he intended, Zek reached her, his arm slipping naturally about her waist, his other hand covering her brow.

'Are you feeling ill, Lizzie?'

The genuine frowning concern in his eyes shook her to the core, and for a moment she blinked up at him feeling as shy as a child. 'No, I . . . only tired, sir.'

'You work too hard girl. I never expected a slave. I saw you out there in that damned garden. The sun is too hot for you, Lizzie. You shouldn't do it.'

She was astonished by the suppressed fury in his voice, and stiffened in his grip. 'You don't . . . I am your employee, sir, and must work for my living. I enjoy gardening. I had little chance to work in a garden in London.'

'Not even in the workhouse?' But all the anger was gone, and he smiled lazily down at her, suddenly squeezing her against his side before releasing her altogether. 'But as your employer I have a certain liberty to order you about, and I am ordering you now to go and lie down for a few hours. Mind, I shall ask Mary if you did!'

'Mr Gray, really, I—'

His smile grew grim. 'Lizzie.'

She turned and marched from the room, slamming the door behind her.

He was not at dinner, so she had to keep all her frustrated comments to herself. Mary said he had gone over to the nearest town for some meeting of the district's land-holders, and would not return until late. Lizzie thought he at least might have told her, so that she could mention it to the kitchen. The thought set her brooding, and she grumbled at him inwardly, not admitting to herself how glad she was to find something to hate him for, after the rather unsettling concern of the afternoon.

He had acted as if . . . as if her cold distance were all a game he was willing to go along with, to play

with her, unless something important occurred,
like her being ill. And then the game was finished
and he'd come and hold her and treat her just as he
had treated her the night of the spider. Was it a
game she was playing? The thought puzzled her,
and she went apprehensively to her bed.

Time went by. Lizzie did her best, which she decided was rather good. She enjoyed being housekeeper, even if she was lonely. It was a lofty, lonely
position, she told herself. She must expect that.
And yet sometimes she would wake from dreams,
tears drying on her cheeks, in which she had played
a part totally different from the drab housekeeper.
Only she didn't remember what it was.

Jessie Grant continued to hate her, though she
kept it hidden under that efficient exterior, and,
really, Lizzie could make no complaints about her
meals. The cooking and preparation was excellent.
The other servants she managed well enough. They
deferred to her higher position, and if they felt
anything for her under their masks they hid it well.
Most of the girls who worked around the kitchen
and the dairy, were assignees, which Lizzie had
learnt meant they were convict girls assigned by the
Government to work for Zek Gray for a certain
time, until they were either given their ticket-of-
leave, or misbehaved and were returned to the
Government.

There were convict men too, who worked about
the place, but mainly the men were ticket-of-leave
men or free labourers. Ralph Grant was the fore-
man, and Lizzie often received a smile from him.
He seemed a nice man, and even took time to chat
to her, bringing out her own tentative smile, and
making her feel almost welcome.

'Mr Gray acts on impulse, you might say,' he told her, one afternoon, when she had met him on the verandah. 'He hired you on impulse. He bought this place on impulse, and he's built it up into something remarkable.'

Lizzie let her gaze follow his out over the paddocks. Perhaps he was right, perhaps Zek Gray was a remarkable man. He certainly worked hard. But did that excuse him for being such a despicable rake?

Ralph cleared his throat, and Lizzie wondered uneasily if something of her feelings had shown on her face. But he wasn't looking at her. He reached into his waistcoat pocket for his tobacco pouch, changed his mind, and shuffled his feet.

'Of course, a man like that creates talk, Miss Banister. Can't help but talk about him. You shouldn't believe all you hear. We're all influenced by likes and dislikes, aren't we? I always find it better to make my own judgments about people.'

'Yes.' Her brown eyes flickered to him almost shyly. 'You seem to like him, Mr Grant. Not just as an employer, but for himself.'

He nodded. 'Aye, I do, Miss Banister.'

Lizzie wondered if the poor man realised his wife was in love with the master he so admired. She liked him suddenly, and wished she could like his wife as well. But Jessie Grant had put that feeling well beyond her reach. So her smile was friendly when he took his leave of her, and he afterwards told a silently furious Jessie that he thought Miss Banister a sweet girl.

Angelica came again, but Lizzie didn't see her. She went in search of Zek, and by the smile on her pink mouth when she rode by, Lizzie knew whatever ploy she had used had been successful. Somehow this made her angry—the thought of that poor old man being deceived, she told herself—and when Zek came in for his dinner she glared at him.

He looked rather irritated himself, and barely murmured a civil good evening to her.

'Did Mrs Bailey find you?' she said sweetly, glancing at him. 'Mary said she was looking for you.'

His eyes narrowed, but he said evenly enough, 'She found me.'

'I meant to offer her refreshment, but she didn't come into the house. It must have been quite urgent.'

After a moment he said, 'She thought so.'

And what one must make of that, Lizzie decided later, the Lord alone knew.

One evening he went out to dinner at the Baileys', and didn't return until early morning. Lizzie heard him come in, his boots a little unsteady on the floor. She hoped he had a headache in the morning, and lay smiling darkly to herself. But other than a rather pale cast to his features he showed no signs of outward suffering over the breakfast table.

'Did you enjoy your evening out, sir,' she dared, making her smile coolly pleasant.

He eyed her rather balefully. 'I did, Miss Banister. Angelica's dinners are always worth attending, for their amusement value anyway. Quite scandalous, sometimes. I won't soil your ears with examples.'

But her own eyes narrowed, and seeing that he smiled.

'Does that upset your puritan notions of the way things should be, Miss Banister? It shouldn't. After all, thinking about something and doing something are much the same, aren't they? Some people think, some do.'

'And Mrs Bailey does, Mr Gray? Is that what you're saying?'

He laughed quietly. 'Haven't you heard about Angelica's favourite pastime? Men, Miss Banister, in a word. She has played fast and loose with every man below fifty within two hundred miles of here. And yet . . .' he considered her ever widening eyes. '. . . I think I could keep her in line. If I had a mind to, that is.'

'You deserve each other!' she spat, her face flushing, her eyes gleaming with hatred and rage and misery.

He saw only the hatred, and laughed softly. 'I was beginning to wonder where she was. The *real* Lizzie Banister. I began to fear that polite, colourless creature had overcome her altogether.'

'You're loathsome.'

'In short, a toad. Toads *can* be loathsome, I suppose. But surely, Lizzie, there are some good toads?'

She clenched her hands until the nails dugs into her palms, glaring at him over the polished surface of the dining-room table. After a moment will triumphed over emotion, and she allowed herself to relax a little. Smiling, arrogant devil! She would not listen to him.

'And perhaps we do deserve each other,' he mused. 'Angelica and I. I do admit my reputation is not all that it could be. I like a pretty ankle, the same as most men, and I'm not averse to a little dalliance, if both parties know the rules of the game. I don't purposefully break hearts, Lizzie.'

You've broken mine. The words formed so clearly in her mind she blinked in astonishment. She couldn't . . . she didn't . . . Oh Lord, but she did! She loved the creature! She was in love with a drawling, conceited, handsome, arrogant lecher.

'By the way,' he went on, as if something momentous had not just occurred, 'as I'm considering marriage so seriously of late, I think it might be an idea to do some redecorations. I want you to take a look around, decide if you think anything needs painting up. New furnishings and the like.'

She stared at her plate, trying to get a grip on the waves of misery threatening to flood her.

'Why bother asking me?' she muttered gruffly, retreating behind the shield from her vulnerability. 'Why not ask Angelica Bailey? I'm sure she would love to come and look over the house. I'm sure she has wonderful taste, too.'

'But I'm asking you, Lizzie. You are my housekeeper, aren't you?'

She was that. She could not refute the insidious voice on that count. She felt a little like weeping. He was asking her to prepare the house for when he could bring Angelica here, asking *her*, who had suddenly discovered she loved him.

In the midst of her jumbled thoughts, she heard him stand, his chair sliding back, and the sound of his boots coming around towards her own chair. He must never know, How he would roar! Plain old Lizzie Banister, the girl he half-despised, half-pitied, in love with him. It was amusing, but in such a miserable way she could not laugh. It took the residue of her courage to fling up her head and glare at him with all the old, fierce hatred. He laughed, looking down at her.

'I hope you fall off your horse,' she hissed.

He put out a hand, and before she could move,

snatched out the pins that held her severe chignon in place. Her hair fell down her back, wave upon unruly wave, suddenly softening the sharpness of her features. Her mouth dropped open, and he kindly closed it with a tap under her chin.

'That's better,' he said, stroking the flesh a moment, head to one side as he considered her. 'I've been meaning to do that for ages.' He smiled into her glittering eyes. 'Ah, it's refreshing talking to you, Lizzie! No simpering, no grovelling. Just unadorned loathing.'

Stuttering, she began trying to repair the damage. But he was already gone. She gave up then, and slumped over her plate, wondering why such a thing had to happen to her. To plain, clumsy, foolish Lizzie, who had never had a proposal in her life, and whose one experience of seduction, before Zek Gray took her in hand, was a drunken kiss in the corridor of a London town house.

And now, Zek Gray had turned her life upside down. She spent her time swinging from bewildering desire to red rages, and back again. She had been prey to jealousy and night-time weepings, tenderness and uncontrollable fury. He had made her life a misery and now, to top it all off, she was in love with him! Well, they said women were always fools over rakes; something to do with the fact that their wickedness made one want to tame them. After all, the woman who trained a rake to heel must be some woman!

Not that Lizzie expected to tame Zek Gray. He was totally beyond her comprehension in almost everything he did. Why had he spoken to her about marrying Angelica Bailey, and the next moment pulled the pins from her hair? It made no sense, none of it.

'What will I do?' she whispered softly, and blinked blindly at her plate.

'Miss Banister?'

She started. Mary had come in softly. The girl's eyes were on her, and for a moment Lizzie thought she surprised sympathy in them, before she had hidden whatever expression they held behind her servant's trained blankness.

'Mary, take the breakfast things back to the kitchen, please.'

'Yes, Miss Banister.'

'Mr Gray tells me he wishes to redecorate the house.'

Her eyes widened.

'He is thinking of getting married, he says.'

Mary's eyes popped even more. She swallowed, 'But . . . who to, Miss?'

Lizzie shrugged, and glanced away, pushing ineffectually at her hair. After a moment she became aware of a hand on her shoulder.

Mary's eyes were warm. 'Miss Banister, you mustn't think . . . I mean, men being what they are . . . I mean, he'll come around, I'm sure . . .'

She meant well, though she had the wrong idea altogether if she thought Lizzie was hoping to wed Zek Gray. But Lizzie smiled and said, kindly, 'You're very thoughtful, Mary. Don't . . . don't tell the others I spoke. I was a little upset, I think, and . . .'

The girl nodded, and bobbing a curtsy went out.

The house could certainly do with work, Lizzie decided, as she cast her keen eye around it for the first time in the light of a prospective bride. If it were she who was coming here to live, she would remove that panelling for a start, and . . . yes, and re-cover those chairs in green. Something cool.

Perhaps a rug here, before the fireplace, and that dreadful lacy thing over the curtains could come down! The work kept her occupied most of the day, and even Jessie's watchful blue eyes couldn't disturb her.

At dinner, she launched out on a long monologue about what needed doing and what she had to say about this and that. He listened thoughtfully, without looking at her, and in the end nodded.

'Yes, I can see it as you say. I'll get Ralph in tomorrow and we can see about hiring the necessary labour. I'll get some stuff sent up from Bathurst, too.' He looked at her, a thin smile curling his mouth lopsidedly. 'Thank you, Lizzie. You've done a thoroughly fine job.'

She nodded, pretending sudden interest in her meal. 'I hope your . . . bride will be pleased, sir. Perhaps you should ask her to come and look, I mean, in case she doesn't like my suggestions.'

But he shook his head, and his eyes were suddenly quite expressionless. 'I think not, Lizzie. I want it to be a surprise, you see.'

She did see. Or tried to. The fact that the thought of Angelica's smile of happiness, the excitement in her blue eyes when he brought her in, still dressed in her white bridal gown, made Lizzie physically ill was beside the point. She put that all to one side, and concentrated on her meal. After a time she was even able to ask him about the wheat crop, and listen to his remarks with a certain interest.

Afterwards, she did some stitchery in the sitting-room, while he prowled the room, glass in hand, making her nervous. He stood behind her chair once, and the hairs on the back of her neck prickled because of it. She had to bite her lip to prevent herself from telling him to go away.

Was marriage to Angelica so disturbing to him, and if so, why did he pretend he wanted to marry her? Lizzie gave up trying to fathom his thoughts; they were quite incomprehensible to her. She would be thanking God it was not *she* he was marrying, if she didn't love him so.

A knock on the door startled them, and at Zek's yell to enter, Ralph appeared.

'Mr Gray,' he said, with a brief smile to Lizzie, 'just thought you'd like to know one of the convict men is gone. Jessie says one of the kitchen girls gave him food and a jacket this afternoon. She's down in the office. I thought you'd want to question her.'

'Of course.'

He put his glass down, and went out. Lizzie sat a moment, wondering if anything was expected of her, and if so, what. But after a time Zek Gray returned.

'Have you found him?' she asked.

He shook his head, moodily gazing out of the window into the night. 'The girl didn't know where he was going, but I've an idea it'd be Bathurst. Poor devil. Anyway, we'll get after him in the morning. I suppose this'll mean the magistrate will have to be informed, and all the rest.'

'Why did he run away?' she asked softly. 'It seems to me . . . it seems to me you are not a harsh taskmaster, sir.'

He shrugged. 'I suppose there are men who can't abide containment at any price. I do try to make it . . . comfortable. I've known some who don't even feed their men the regulation amounts, and then expect them to work like galley-slaves. I always try to do what I can.'

Something about his manner was so downhearted, Lizzie felt her hands itching to hold and comfort him. She bit her lip, but he happened to look up at that moment and caught her eye—she wondered afterwards if he had not perhaps done it all on purpose.

The old mockery was dancing in his own black eyes, and he said in a soft, loathsomely drawling voice, 'Feeling sorry for me, Lizzie? There's no need. I've done my best and there's no more I *can* do.'

'But you feel responsible.'

An eyebrow rose in the old way. 'Yes, I feel responsible. You're very perceptive, Miss Banister.'

She ignored that. 'Is there any way in which I can help, sir?'

He grinned. 'Well now . . .' But the grin faded and he shook his head, as if thinking better of what he had been about to say. 'No, there's nothing you can do, thank you, Lizzie. Go off to bed.'

She rose, her shoulders rigid. 'You're always telling me that! As though I'm a . . . a child!'

His laughter was soft. 'Is that so? Perhaps it's because I prefer to think of you as one. It's safer that way, isn't it? If I start thinking of you as a grown woman again, Lizzie-mine, even your acid tongue may not save you.'

The look in his eyes frightened her so much she could hardly get out her goodnight, and rushed out of the room as if all the devils in hell were after her.

To mull over what he had meant seemed pointless when she understood him so little. He could be teasing her again, or taunting her—he may even be serious. Perhaps she represented a challenge to his seductive powers? It only made her more than ever certain that he must never, never discover how hopelessly she loved him.

The following morning Zek was already gone, and she was glad to breakfast alone. He spent the day out, looking for the man, and then, when he couldn't be found, riding into town to speak with the magistrate there and put out a description of the escapee.

'What will happen to him?' Lizzie asked Ralph Grant, when the latter bid her good day as she was working in the garden.

'Flogging,' Ralph said. 'But I suppose Mr Gray will be lenient, and maybe not make a complaint. Flogging is the best that can happen to him. If he gets back to Sydneyton, or Bathurst, he'll be put on the road gang. He's not a bad one, only a bit reckless I think.'

It sounded inhuman, but Lizzie said nothing. Zek *was* a good master. He did care for his employees. Once she would have scorned the idea that a man like that could be honourable in his way. In fact she had believed only 'gentlemen', with their carefully-worded conversation, and glum faces, and impeccable morals—at least on the surface of their lives—were honourable. But Zek was none of those things, and Zek was a man to be admired. She was suddenly absurdly proud of him.

'He's a bad one,' Cook had once told her, concerning a certain guest in the household. 'But his father's a Duke, so he's invited everywhere. Wickedness can be ignored in a Duke's son, Banister.'

'It seems unfair,' Lizzie had ventured. 'I mean, if he's bad . . .'

'Well the world is set down in a certain way, Banister, and we must abide by its rules.'

But why! Lizzie had thought, though dared not voice it beneath Cook's stern gaze.

'Just you don't get yourself alone with him, that's

all,' the cook added, maliciously wounding the plum pudding batter with her wooden spoon. 'Luckily you're a plain girl. You don't have to watch yourself like some others I could name. But this Duke's son, Banister, he's not so fussy . . . from what I hear!'

'You nasty old bat,' Lizzie said aloud, and clapped her hand over her mouth, as if Cook were really in the room with her and not just in her head. But even so the words had shocked her a little. She had disagreed with something Cook said. In fact, since meeting Zek Gray she had disagreed with lots of Cook's teachings, and rebelled against the rest. Her ideas of right and wrong had been turned topsy-turvy. Perhaps she was being corrupted?

It was quite warm in the garden, and the afternoon sun beat down on the ground a little more mercilessly than she had expected. But she needed the occupation to clear her mind, and bent to her work with a will. She tried to empty her thoughts of all but the delicate task of planting the seedlings she had sprouted, and pressing the soil about their stems. She was so busy with her work that she didn't hear the hoof beats until they were upon her, and when the arm scooped down, like an iron band about her middle, she could do no more than scream and cling on.

The ground tilted, and then she was tumbled unceremoniously on to the front of the saddle, gripped quite roughly against a warm, familiar chest, her heart thudding, her breath gasping as the world righted itself.

Shock was uppermost. She seemed all out of order. Her hair tumbling down, her skirts bundled up, showing a good length of stockinged leg and a button-up boot. And then the fact that he was

grinning, so obviously pleased with himself, fed her
rage until she began to wriggle furiously in his grip.
Admiration and pride for him were quite forgotten!

He drew up Star, laughing, and looked down into
her furious little face.

'Put me down!'

'Lizzie—'

'At once!' she hissed, eyes blazing.

He sighed, some of the laughter vanishing, and
she slid down to the ground. Her eyes flashed, and
she lifted her chin to gaze up at him, her hands
naturally gravitating to her hips in an attitude of
righteous rage.

'How dare you frighten me so? How dare you
treat me like a . . . like a . . . How dare you! Isn't it
bad enough that everyone thinks I'm your . . . your
mistress, without adding fuel to the fire? Isn't it bad
enough that I have to put up with everyone
laughing and whispering behind my back, without
you treating me so?'

The laughter had all gone now. He looked grave,
his eyes almost rueful, and he dismounted to stand
beside her. She narrowed her own eyes at him, and
stepped back, uneasily aware that she should never
have spoken so to him; and she would not have
done, if he had not frightened her witless.

'Do they really think so?' he said in a deceptively
quiet, light tone. She saw the gleam of battle in the
darkness of his eyes, and the grim line of his jaw.

'Not to my face perhaps, although . . . but I can
feel it. I have no friends here, except perhaps Mary
and . . . and Ralph. Everyone else despises me for
what they think I am. Perhaps if I . . . I were openly
what they imagine, it would not be so bad, but they
believe I am a hypocrite to boot!'

'Lizzie, I'm sorry.' He did look contrite, flicking

her a look up through his thick lashes. 'I only meant to teach you a lesson for disobeying my orders. You shouldn't work in the sun. If I've made things worse for you, then forgive me. But you are the house-keeper here. You must show them your authority.'

Authority! What was the use of that, when her position here was such a sham? And now that Mary had guessed her love for him, they would probably pity her as well!

Perhaps he saw something of the misery in her eyes, for suddenly he brushed his finger down her cheek.

'Cheer up! Why not come into town with me?'

'Thank you, no,' she whispered, standing rigidly before him.

'Lizzie . . .'

'I hate you for doing this to me!'

'Indeed, Lizzie, sometimes I think you must.' Anger lit his eyes now, and she was sorry for putting it there. It was a dangerous, reckless sort of anger. As if he had decided on a course of action and meant to carry it through no matter what.

He came towards her, and she backed away. Out here they were quite open to the watchful eyes of all and sundry, and Lizzie did not want to be the cause of any more gossip this morning.

'If everyone already believes you are my mis-tress, as you so delicately put it, then what can anything we do matter? We are in a way immune to them, aren't we?'

His reasoning was faulty. She knew it, but couldn't for a moment find an argument. He caught her arm, and dragged her up against him. His mouth fastened on hers, brutally forcing a re-sponse. His other hand slid over her body with a thoroughness she found horrifying in the circumstances. He let her go almost at once, breathing fast, his eyes daring her to retaliate.

Her lips hurt, and she put a hand to them, staring at him with wide, accusing eyes. 'Why?' she whispered.

The lines on his face deepened. 'I wanted there to be no doubt whatsoever,' he told her coldly. 'You can't back out then, Lizzie, can you?'

Back out of what? 'I don't understand,' she wailed, and turning began to run blindly back towards the house.

She half expected to feel him grab her again, but he let her go. Tears kept filling her eyes, and her skirts hampered her, but somehow she found her way inside to her room and threw herself down on the bed, sobbing as if her heart would break. She remained there a long time, working at clearing her mind and emotions of all thought of him and her own wicked longings, and when she finally managed to face the household, it was evening.

Jessie met her on the verandah, blue eyes carefully veiled, though Lizzie heard the glee in her voice.

'Mr Gray informed me he will be away until late tonight, Miss Banister, and not to wait dinner for him. He has gone to the Baileys'.'

Lizzie thought she retained her composure very well, though she had to pretend for a moment that there was a piece of earth still clinging to her sleeve, and brushed at it meticulously.

'Indeed,' she said.

Jessie had evidently been a witness to the wild embrace, and her subsequent rush away from Zek, and drawn her own conclusions.

'It's a shame about Mrs Bailey,' Jessie went on smoothly. 'Her man bein' a cripple, an' all. She's the sort as needs a real man in her life. Mr Gray always seems ready to fill the role.'

Lizzie's chin came up, and she looked into Jessie's eyes, her own cold as ice. Jessie looked away, flushing a little, and muttered a few words about things to do before departing.

So he had gone to Angelica. Lizzie nodded. Yes, he would marry Angelica, just as he had said he would, and Lizzie would leave. She could not stay now, could she? Life was bad enough, but after that . . . Perhaps that had been his intention, when he insulted her so before the whole world—it had seemed like the whole world at the time. Perhaps he had meant to make her life so unbearable she would go away and leave him in peace. But it had been he who brought her here! And he who sometimes treated her as if she were a lovely and desirable woman.

She ate little for dinner, and sat alone in the dining-room, staring at the long windows. She kept thinking of them together, Angelica and Zek Gray. She imagined Angelica's white body, as eager and twisting as a snake, and Zek . . . white hands clutching his black hair, the sound of their laughter. It was suddenly quite unbearable.

She started up as if to run, gazing about her blindly. She saw the decanter quite by accident, and for a moment stared at it. Zek liked a drop of brandy in the evenings. Sometimes he drank too much. She remembered his unsteady footsteps the night of the Baileys' dinner. With sudden decision she walked over to the table and poured herself some of the liquor in the best crystal glass she could find. She swallowed it quickly, pulling a face.

The heat of it burned down her throat, warming

her stomach. She drank again, taking it like medicine. After a moment she felt quite light-headed, and much better. She poured herself a full glass and went to sit by the window, brooding into the darkness.

How dared he treat her as he had? How dared he make havoc of her life because it suited his vanity, his conceit? 'I like a pretty ankle the same as most men'. What arrogance! And now he was angry with her, just because she had stuck up for her principles and refused to be seduced. Perhaps that was why he wanted to get rid of her so badly? A woman refusing to fall into his arms was bad for his reputation. It was so unfair . . .

'I'll never give myself to any man,' she muttered, and clapped a hand over her mouth at the sound of her own belligerent voice. She took another swig from the glass, blinking. Even Cook had a nip of brandy every once in a while. It was good for you, she used to say. Well, what was good for Cook was good for Lizzie!

The room was a little odd, tilting like a ship's cabin. She wondered for a moment if they were afloat, knowing such a thing impossible but not totally rejecting it.

'I'm worn out,' she said, nodding her head. 'Slaving for that . . . that toad.'

A tear rolled down her cheek, tasting salty on her lips. The trouble was, she thought drearily, she wished she *was* his mistress. Despite the fact that he was a womanising lecher, a handsome, feckless devil, she wanted to be his mistress. The fact that her conventional, proper soul was shocked to the core by this admission did not prevent her from realising it was a fact. She wanted to lie abed with him, and comfort him, and be all the things

Angelica was to him. She wanted to be beautiful, and gentle, and . . . and . . .

Another tear rolled down her cheek, but she brushed it aside. What had he said, when that hussy had waved at them out of the window at Bathurst? 'I can see you wearing that'. And on the ship, 'I can see you in blue silk'—Disgusting! She glanced down at her grey gown, plucking at the coarse stuff of the skirt. After a moment she stood up, a trifle unsteadily, and went purposefully into her bedroom.

She had been busy stitching a nightgown for Jane. A lovely, delicate thing with lace at hem and neckline and a blue ribbon threaded through the bodice just below the bosom. It was the sort of feminine, dainty thing Jane would look beautiful in and that Lizzie had never before dared to wear or even think of herself as wearing. She had always thought coarse, sacklike garments good enough for herself—had rarely even envied Jane. Until now.

Another tear ran down her face, and she sipped from the glass, almost missing her lips. 'Not fair,' she whispered. 'Why can't I be pretty and little and . . . and . . .'

She touched the soft material, and then with sudden clumsy decision began to undress. It took several moments and a number of false starts before she had completed her task, and was able to view herself with a slightly glazed vision. The nightgown fitted her quite well, considering it had been for Jane's shorter, plumper figure. She fumbled at the pins in her hair, raking it out over her shoulders. She peered at herself, leaning forward to see better. She looked quite pretty, in a blowzy sort of way, she decided.

She was too tall, of course, and too slim. Long

legs, though. She tried to compose her features into an enticing smile. She bit her lips, as she had seen Jane do, to redden them, and pouted at herself.

'As good . . . as good as anyone,' she told herself, and took another drink of brandy, lifting the glass to salute her reflection. 'To principles,' she muttered.

Someone moved behind her. A shadow, near the door. She turned in vague surprise, and saw she had not closed it properly. Zek Gray's astonished face stared back at her from the darkness of the hall. He seemed unable to believe his eyes, and stood staring at her scantily-clad figure for quite some time, while she swayed, and leaned heavily against the foot of the bed to keep her balance. The movement seemed to bring him abruptly to his senses. He shut the door, quietly, to ensure their complete privacy.

'Lizzie, what in God's name are you up to?' His voice was soft, but harsh with astonishment and anger.

Why was he angry? She almost fell over, and glared back at him sullenly, her mouth drooping. Something in the look was very seductive, and he caught his breath.

'Lizzie, are you all right?' A step closer brought him in range of the brandy fumes, and he noted the glass. His eyebrows shot up, almost disappearing into the hairline, and he folded his arms. 'That's it, is it? Drunk?'

Her toes curled on the floor, and she let her head fall on to her chest, dark hair swinging forward to hide her face. 'I thought you were with Angelica. Where . . . why did you go there?' she demanded belligerently, and a tear ran down her cheek. 'And why did you come back? I thought—'

'I went to speak to her on a private matter, Lizzie. None of your concern. And the reason I'm back early is that I finished earlier than I expected.'

She sniffed.

'One would think, Lizzie, you wished I hadn't come back at all.'

'I know you hate me,' she burst out. 'I know you do.'

He looked surprised. 'Do you indeed?' His voice was quiet.

She pushed at her hair, her fingers tangling. She frowned, trying to pull free, and he came forward and took her wrist gently in his hand. 'Here, let me.' He smelt of tobacco. He smelt, too, of perfume. Angelica's.

'Why didn't you stay with her,' she hissed, staggering as the room tilted again, and falling against his chest. 'Stay with her, I don't care.'

He freed her hand, and stood holding her fingers in his own. She glanced at him uncertainly and cleared her throat. She seemed to realise suddenly that she was wearing a négligé, and frowned down at herself, her other hand plucking at the lace on the bodice. It was much too low cut—indecently so—and the swell of her bosom showed over the top, even as her figure showed plainly through the material of the skirt. The brandy effects cleared enough for her to feel a faint shock at her actions, and she cleared her throat again, trying to draw her hand away from his. He tilted up her chin and looked down into her eyes. She felt for a moment as if she were drowning, and gazed back dizzily.

'Lizzie,' his voice was soft, 'why did you drink so much of my brandy? Were you so unhappy?'

'Yes!'

He smiled faintly, his dark eyes gleaming with

amusement and more that she dared not analyse. 'Because of what I did this morning?'

'I hate you both. You and . . . and Angelica. I hate you all.'

His fingers tightened on her chin. 'I didn't mean to make you unhappy. I meant to put it all right. I still do. I've told Angel so. Lizzie, I want to marry you.'

She shook her head, her eyes wide and muzzy. Her head felt dreadful, full of cotton wool, and she could have sworn her feet were floating some feet above the floor. He was trying to trick her, he must be. But he was looking at her with such a soft, warm look in his eyes. She watched his face come closer, and felt the brush of his lips on hers.

'I want to marry you, Lizzie,' he said again. 'That's why I did what I did this morning. I mean to make everything up to you, and I wanted to make quite sure you couldn't back out.'

'I've got principles,' she murmured.

That, however, didn't seem to deter him. He drew her closer into his arms, holding her as if she were porcelain. He kissed her again, deeper this time, and when he drew away she leaned against him, her lips following his.

'Principles,' she breathed, and felt him laughing.

'Lizzie,' he said in a harsh vice, 'you're playing with fire.'

Her eyes filled with tears. 'Zek,' she said, 'I don't want to be burned.'

He stroked her cheek, making soothing noises, while his eyes shone with something very unsoothing. They glowed, making her feel dizzy and flushed. She bowed her head again, and felt him kiss her temple, nuzzling aside her hair, his lips shifting to her ear, her cheek, seeking her mouth.

'I know,' he murmured, 'you've been unhappy. Everything'll be all right though, Lizzie. Everything'll be all right when we're married. The talk will stop, Lizzie, you'll see, and you will be accepted as my wife. And as for me . . .' his laughter tickled her skin. 'Well, I will be able to relax, too, won't I? There hasn't been much of that for me, Lizzie Banister, since you've been here.'

She hardly heard him. 'Do you like my night-gown?' she whispered.

'Most fetching,' he said, and there was laughter in his voice.

'I knew you would! I knew it.'

'Well that's wonderful. Now, go back to bed. Come on, like a good girl.'

She looked up, her eyes smiling, her mouth wide with her smile. 'You're treating me like a child again,' she reminded him.

He caught his breath, tightening his hold on her. 'And you're treating me like a tame cat, which by God I am not!'

He began to kiss her almost desperately, and she responded warmly and naturally, hugging him against her as she would never have dared to do had not the brandy weakened her reserve.

'Perhaps it's better this way,' he said, as if to himself. He had begun to take off his jacket and shirt. 'I don't want to frighten you, or hurt you, Lizzie, but usually you're so damned jumpy . . .'

A warning bell rang in her head. She shook it to try and clear it, and had to cling to the bed-end again as she almost fell over.

'What about all the others?' she managed at last, in a far away voice.

'What about them?' he repeated softly, his black

eyes even darker in the shadows of his handsome face.

She watched him stepping lightly towards her, like some big, dangerous cat. Broad shoulders and chest, heavily muscled, trimming down to his waist and hips. Strong legs. He was quite beautiful, and she had to swallow to regain her voice.

'Well . . .' she clung to the brass bed-end. 'I can't possibly measure up to them, can I? I've not had the . . . . the experience.' She glared at him, daring him to comment.

His face was soft with tenderness. 'Lizzie, my little love, I want you just as you are. Can't you see that?'

Absurdly, she knew she was lost then, but kept fighting, going down that third time. 'I mean, I'm not even pretty, and you're used to pretty girls. At least, I suppose you are. And I'm thin and awkward and . . . how could you want to marry me?'

He held out his arms, and she went into them so hard she knocked his breath out with a huff. It seemed to her, afterwards, that it was all part of the dream.

His mouth closed on hers, warm and sweet, and she let her arms slide about his waist, feeling flesh warm and smooth. And strong. He held her so tightly, and yet so gently, it was like being the captive of a friendly storm. And then he had lifted her high against his chest, and was carrying her towards the absurd bed.

His palms came to rest either side of her face, and he looked into her eyes. 'Oh Lizzie,' he said, and bending kissed her lips gently, then passionately.

His mouth teased and touched, and though she twisted away, she held him closer with her arms. His hands stroked and unwound her from her nightgown and found her secrets. Near the end, she was in such a fever of excitement and emotion, she felt completely wanton. Eyes brilliant, hair tumbling riotously about her on the pillows. She gazed up to where he was poised above her.

Perspiration dampened his upper lip, his dark hair fell over his brow, his eyes shone soft and dark. He had never been so handsome to her as he stooped and with extraordinary gentleness, made her his, meeting her trembling cry with a kiss.

'Zek,' she managed, much later, lying still in the curve of his arm, her body pressed trustingly to his.

'Lizzie.'

He turned his cheek to her brow, his hand stroking her arm. He sounded weary, and she thought it took him an effort to act naturally. His face too was strained, and she wondered suddenly if it had been as wonderful an experience for him as it had been for her.

Her lashes swept down to hide her eyes.

'Sleep my love,' he whispered, bending to kiss her lips. 'Sleep.'

And surprisingly, she slept.

CHAPTER
EIGHT

SHE woke alone, and lay a moment wondering if her head was going to come off, or whether it already had. The light from the shutters was like daggers, and she squeezed her eyes shut with a soft groan. It was half an hour before she dared try to get up, and then it took much effort and much groaning before she was dressed. She kept remembering bits and pieces of the night before, and hardly dared to allow the thoughts to come filtering through.

Zek's astonished face, and his kisses, and other things which made her turn pink and white by turns. And something more she hardly dared even to consider was real. Zek asking her to marry him.

She was sitting on the bed, trying to gather enough courage to go out into the house when a knock sounded like an avalanche on her door. She went white, and staggered up, crying for them to stop. Mary peeped in, her face carefully devoid of emotion.

'Mr Gray wishes to see you, Miss Banister, in his office.'

'Thank you, Mary,' she smiled wanly. 'I'll be there directly.'

She made her way by slow degrees to the office, knocking softly on the panels. His voice was too loud, but she gritted her teeth and entered, feeling like a schoolgirl called up before the headmaster.

He was standing by the window, and she blinked as he turned. He was smiling, however, his eyes reading her face correctly. 'Feeling a little out of sorts, Lizzie?' he murmured.

'You look very pleased with yourself,' she retorted sharply, and was sorry for it when her head began to pound.

He came and took her hands. 'Lizzie, do you remember last night?'

She went pink, and bit her lip. 'I don't know. I think . . .'

He laughed softly, making her go pinker than ever. 'Exactly. And apart from that, you agreed to marry me.'

'I . . .' She shook her head, but his grip on her hands tightened. 'Zek, are you sure? I mean . . .'

Can you be faithful, or don't you intend to try? she wanted to ask him. I love you, and if you break my heart I doubt I could bear it, she wanted to cry. But she said neither, standing mute with her head throbbing.

'You said you were unhappy,' he cut in rather sharply. 'I didn't realise the prospect of marriage to me would be equally depressing.'

'Oh no!'

He was frowning, however, his eyes searching her face. 'Surely it would be no worse than your present situation? And besides . . . since we've already anticipated the ceremony—and I don't take virgins for sport my girl, let me tell you!—we have no choice.'

She hung her head, realising then what she had not realised last night. He was marrying her because she had told him they thought her his mistress. Last night he had gone to Angelica and explained matters to her, and then returned to tell Lizzie his decision. No argument of hers could have moved him. He did not love her. He never had. She had offered her body and he being what he was had taken it. She could not blame him for that. But the facts hurt. They hurt a good deal.

'I will marry you,' she said dully. 'Of course I will. I must.'

His smile was without humour, and he nodded briefly, releasing her fingers. 'Go and put on your best dress then, and pack a few things in a bag. We'll go in to Bathurst as soon as possible.'

She turned and went out, dragging her feet. She dressed carefully, brushed her hair, and packed her bag. It seemed incredible that this should be happening, and she moved as if it were a dream. Mary, eyes popping, came to help, saying that Mr Gray had told her the good news, and they worked in silence.

'I hope you're very happy, Miss Banister,' she said at last, when they were done. Lizzie nodded, smiled with an effort, and went outside.

He had the gig waiting. Lizzie let him help her up into it, glancing aside at the rather stern profile. They drove for a time in utter silence.

'What did Angelica say?' she managed at last.

His knuckles went white on the reins. 'This is nothing to do with her.'

It was everything to do with her, Lizzie thought. If Angelica had been free there would have been no question of him having to marry Lizzie. Good God, perhaps Angelica approved of all this. Why not? She could picture them together, Angelica laughing and purring, 'It'll make no difference to us, though, darling!' And Zek's brown hands stroking her fair hair, his low laughter, 'God, no! How could I compare Lizzie, poor plain Lizzie, with you!'

She shuddered, drawing his attention back to her. He turned his eyes on her face, raking her stiff, straight figure.

'Are you all right?'

'Yes.'

He eyed her a moment in mockery. 'You hardly look a blushing bride.'

'Should I?'

'Don't be sarcastic, Lizzie, it doesn't suit you. I'm sorry there is no time for a big wedding, but in the circumstances . . .'

'I understand.'

Who would want to show off such a bride as she, when Zek Gray had made himself famous because of dalliances with beauties like Angelica Bailey?

They paused for a noon rest at the same tavern, but Lizzie managed to avoid the girl's eyes and stayed close with Zek while he drank his ale and she her water. She felt better for the time spent in the shade—her head seemed to have resumed its normal size—and managed to make some conversation on the rest of the journey, which he answered cursorily. But at least she made the effort.

Bathurst looked almost familiar to her, as they came down from the surrounding hills into the town. Zek seemed pleased to be there too, and smiled as he swung her down at the York Hotel.

'I'll go and see about a licence,' he told her, when they had taken two rooms. 'Dinner is in about an hour.'

'Yes.'

'I thought it best if we wait until we're actually married before asking for the bridal suite.'

His eyes were wicked, but she avoided them.
When he had gone, she rid herself of a curious,
bright-eyed Mrs O'Driscoll, and lay down on the
bed to try and sleep. She felt quite drained with
emotion at the mere thought of a wedding. Perhaps
she was a romantic after all? But the idea of such a
bloodless contract horrified her. She couldn't help
but remember Jane's glowing face and the joy that
filled the air. How could she contemplate marrying
Zek when he didn't love her? It seemed somehow
wrong, and yet . . . she wanted him. Foolish
perhaps, but she loved him so much she no longer
cared what his feelings were. At least he would be
hers, and she may be allowed to share him with
Angelica.

Over dinner he told her, 'I can get a licence in the
morning and we can be married at two.'

'So quickly?'

His smile mocked her shocked expression. 'Of
course. I can pull some weight when I want to,
Lizzie.'

'Oh.'

'In the morning you can buy yourself a new dress.
Here.' He put some money beside her hand. She
stared at it. 'Take it,' he said impatiently. 'I want
my bride to look like a bride, even if she doesn't
feel like one.'

She took the money, and looking up into his eyes
saw his smile. It was as if in doing so she had given
up her last reservation to what he had already
decided was to be her fate.

She found a dress. Blue silk, with white ruching.
She bought a bonnet to match, and new slippers—
dainty things peeping out from under the wide,
buckram-stiffened hem. She bought new under-
things too, silk and satin, so light and feminine

Lizzie blushed at the sight of them, and her hands shook while she dressed.

She was ready long before two, and sat waiting, feeling her heart thudding with apprehension and excitement. She kept glancing in the mirror by the bed, touching her big, fashionable sleeves, smoothing her gloves, and patting at the strands of hair she had somehow contrived to turn into ringlets bouncing against either side of her face.

Her eyes shone like gold, and she stared at herself, hardly daring to believe it. Today she would marry Zek Gray, whom she loved. It seemed rather a pity that he didn't love her.

He came for her at last, and when she stood up to greet him his eyes took in her finery at a glance. He smiled, a little grimly she thought, but his eyes gleamed as he took her hand.

'You *do* look like a bride, Lizzie.'

He was handsome in formal black jacket and trousers, his shirt collar so white it dazzled her. His hair was brushed neatly too, and he wore a gold watch and chain in his waistcoat pocket. He looked every inch the devil-may-care rake. She put her hand in his, feeling his fingers close on hers. He smiled properly then, and bending slightly kissed her soft lips.

'Is it so bad?' he whispered, but gave her no chance to answer as he urged her out of the door.

The minister had agreed to marry them in his residence. His wife acted as a witness, and Zek had a friend, a red-coated soldier, as best man. The soldier, whose name was Captain Leigh Barrett, looked at Lizzie rather curiously, and she flushed at what she felt his thoughts to be—'Fancy old Zek marrying such a thing as that! What happened to Angelica?'

The service was brief.

Zek drew her into his arms at the end, kissing her lips softly. His whispered, 'Oh Lizzie, I'll try hard to make it all right,' didn't help her confidence much, though she managed to smile back into his eyes.

It was still early, and they had a drink with the minister, while Captain Barrett talked of the government, and Lizzie tried to still the trembling in her hands. Zek seemed relaxed, and laughed a lot afterwards, when they had dinner back at the York Hotel. Lizzie lingered over it as long as possible, but there finally came a time when there was nothing more to do but retire to their room.

It was a new room, large and lavish. Lizzie saw that her things had been removed there. Her brush beside his, her one lonely bottle of perfume-water beside his cologne. It made it all more intimate, somehow. More real. Up until now she could tell herself it was a dream. But to see her things and his side by side turned it into reality.

He was removing his coat. His glance was impatient. 'Take off your bonnet, Lizzie! And your gloves! Or do you intend coming to bed in them?'

'I'm sorry,' she whispered, and began to undress.

She turned her back, unbuttoning the gown, and didn't hear him come over to her until his hands closed on her shoulders. 'Lizzie,' he said, and she felt his lips on her nape, lingering. His arms slid about her waist, pulling her back against his big frame. He held her so tightly for a moment she couldn't breathe. But when he turned her about there was none of the suppressed emotion she had thought she felt in him while she couldn't see him. His smile was lightly mocking, and though his eyes blazed it was only desire she saw in them, not love.

Zek was whistling. The wind buffeted Lizzie's bonnet and she clutched it with one hand as the gig bumped over the long road home. They had left Bathurst this morning after over a week spent sampling the delights of that town. It was a period she would never forget. Thinking of it now, she glanced at his face, her eyes almost glazed with love.

Zek had spent the first days buying her a completely new wardrobe. She might protest in vain. He took no notice. 'You're delightful when you blush,' he mocked, when he presented her with his idea of what a woman's night attire should consist of.

There were gowns and blouses, coats and jackets, shoes and stockings, chemisettes and shifts, and other things which she thought, darkly, he shouldn't know about. All so elegant and perfectly fitting. She had to visit the dressmaker too, and he laughed when she didn't want him to sit and watch her being measured and fitted.

'Lizzie,' he teased her, 'you have an excellent figure. Why do you want to hide it under those awful drab rags?'

'I'm too skinny, Zek, and . . .'

He laughed softly, making her blush again. 'You're not skinny in the places that count.'

He bought her jewellery too. Ear-rings and pendants and brooches all so finely-wrought and feminine she felt almost a changed woman just wearing them. Did he really think of her as being as dainty and lovely as his choice seemed to suggest? Or was he pretending she was Angelica, and buying what would suit her?

But he didn't seem to be pining for Angelica. Not noticeably, anyway. His eyes teased her, watching her delight in it all.

'Money,' he mocked, when she protested about the expense. 'You're my wife, Lizzie. I like to see you in clothes I've bought you. Don't you understand that yet? I want to dress you from head to toe. And speaking of head, I've told you a hundred times how much I hate seeing you with your lovely hair dragged back like a horse's tail. Here . . .'

'But Zek—'

'"But Zek"!' he mocked, and when her hair was tumbling about her, he caught her up, kissing her breathless. That was one of the days she had really believed he felt some affection for her.

He watched her like a hawk, too. It puzzled her, that constant, possessive watchfulness he kept up where she was concerned. As though he expected her suddenly to turn into a butterfly and fly away.

Sometimes, when she woke in the morning, he would be lying there awake, watching her. And though he yawned and smiled, as though he too had just awoken, she knew he had been awake for much longer.

She began to wonder if he was regretting his marriage already, and beginning to hate her. His watchful look made her nervous, and frightened of what he might see. She knew that she loved him more than ever, more than was decent, in her opinion, brought up as she had been with fixed ideas on what marriage should properly entail. If she was just a momentary distraction, until he could get back to Angelica, it would just have to serve as a happy memory to colour the rest of her unhappy life.

They dined out with others only once. Captain

Barrett came with his wife to the York. It was with a shock that Lizzie recognised the pretty brunette Zek had kissed ages ago, when they had stayed here, and she glanced at him in astonishment, tempered with a growing outrage. Had he actually gone so far as to seduce his friend's wife?

But Captain Barrett was friendly, and though the brunette seemed to enjoy flirting with Zek, while he laughed at her indulgently, Lizzie could see nothing sinister in their relationship.

'I've known Zek forever,' said the brunette, whose name was Prudence though they called her by her nickname of 'Kitten'.

'Kitten and Leigh are old friends,' Zek murmured in his lazy voice. He caught Lizzie's repressive look and let the laughter glow in his eyes as he raised his glass to her.

Kitten snuggled up against him, wriggling, Lizzie thought privately, like a cat with fleas. Her mouth was blatantly pouting, but Zek only laughed. Leigh guffawed too, and poured himself another drink. Lizzie eyed him rather scornfully. No wonder his wife made up to other men, if her own husband was more interested in his drink.

But after all Captain Barrett had another interest. Lizzie.

Zek had ordered them a private room, and after they had dined there, they drank champagne among the rather awesomely opulent furnishings. Sheer luxury, Lizzie thought, big-eyed, looking about her. Who would have thought Lizzie Banister would ever be dining in such a place?

'To Lizzie!' the captain said, raising his glass.

Zek drank, and Kitten waved her glass without attempting to salute the other woman, her eyes gleaming with jealousy. What was it about Zek

Gray, Lizzie sighed, that brought out the very worst in women? They made fools of themselves over him while he sat and let them.

'You know, Lizzie,' the captain went on in his abrupt way, 'you're a damned fine woman. Damned fine.'

Lizzie flushed, trying to laugh it off, but the captain wouldn't be side-tracked. Kitten was rubbing her face on Zek's shoulder, her eyes hectic.

'Damned fine,' he repeated. 'I reckon Zek here's a damned lucky man.'

'Damned lucky,' Zek murmured, and winked at her over Kitten's smooth *coiffure*.

'Oh Zek,' Kitten murmured, and Lizzie saw with outrage that the other woman's hand was running over his chest, while her pink tongue darted into his ear. He was enjoying it too, the toad!

With sudden blind determination, Lizzie turned to the captain and smiled. He blinked at her, and after a moment smiled back, a light she couldn't mistake coming into his rather protuberant blue eyes.

'That colour suits you, Lizzie,' he said with approval, eyeing her bosom where it showed over the neckline of her gown.

Zek had chosen it. It was red, a deep, blood-red, and showed off her white skin and dark hair and eyes to some advantage. She had protested it was too low at the front and too tight in most other places. He had laughed at her, and from the look on his face when he had viewed her in it tonight she knew he approved.

Lizzie smiled at the captain, allowing her hand to pause over his shoulder, before resting her fingers lightly on the insignia on his red jacket. 'It suits you too, Captain. I always think a uniform so . . . so distinguished.'

Maybe it was the wine, or anger and wine both, but suddenly she felt quite as outrageously flirtatious as Kitten. Her fingers smoothed the captain's well-cut coat, and she smiled at him, fluttering her lashes.

'Zek's been my friend for more years now than I care to name,' he said, meeting her look, 'but damn, ma'am, if I don't wish he weren't! Damn, if I don't. Friendship can be a damned nuisance sometimes, Lizzie, eh?'

His hand slipped about her trim waist, and he squeezed her rather more enthusiastically than was comfortable. Her eyes slid around to the other couple. Kitten was still murmuring sweet nothings in Zek's ear, but Zek himself was watching her. And his face was like thunder.

The party broke up after that. He was barely civil in his goodbyes, though fortunately the Barretts were rather too buoyed up with wine to notice.

They had hardly reached the bedroom when he pushed her back against the door and began to kiss her with a savage single-mindedness that sapped all protests. His hands slid over hips and breasts, bruising tender flesh as though he meant to hurt . . .

'That's to remind you whose wife you are,' he said breathlessly, staring into her face, his own pale and sharp with some hitherto unseen emotion. 'And remember it, Lizzie!'

'Zek!' she gasped, and then, eyes narrowing, 'Why shouldn't I flirt? I didn't see you pushing that . . . that woman away!'

'You didn't see me urging her on, either, did you?'

'I wasn't urging anyone on! Besides . . .' and her eyes grew sly, 'I thought he was sweet.'

He caught her arm as she went to walk away into the room, and swung her around against him. His eyes were ablaze and she felt fear before his kiss shut it out. His hands were tangling in her hair, raking it down so that the pins fell to the floor like rain. Lizzie squealed, struggling to escape, but he held her, tugging her head back so that he could further his exploration of her long throat and half-naked bosom.

Her fingers were shaking as she tried to tug his head away, shaking as much with the strain of wanting him to go on as wanting him to stop.

'Zek!'

He looked up then, frowning. His eyes delved deep into hers, and read there the truth. After a moment he relaxed into laughter. The rage was gone as if it had never been. His mouth curled, his eyes narrowed wickedly, and he stepped back.

'So that was it, eh?' He pinched her cheek in an almost brotherly fashion. 'You minx. But don't ever let me see you acting that way again, hear?'

The smile remained on his mouth, his stance was relaxed, but looking into his eyes she saw the order, and the anger, and turned nervously away.

'I will if I want to,' Lizzie muttered, like a rebellious child, and shrugged one shoulder.

'Oh will you now? Well I warn you, this is what you can expect by way of retaliation.' He swung her around against him, and then tossed her on to the bed as easily as if she had been thistledown. Lizzie squealed, trying to clamber up, but he was already beside her, struggling to pinion her hands.

It was the work of a minute to capture and subdue her. He gazed down into her flushed face as she squirmed half-heartedly. Her hair was quite untameable, her gown indecently low from the fight. His eyes, brilliant with triumph, darkened to desire. She saw the demon come leaping, and was still as he bent. Her lips parted of their own accord before he reached them. His kiss was tender, but urgent. Her hands, free now, crept around his nape and pulled him closer.

He began to undo the hooks and eyes on her bodice, kissing the flesh as each inch was revealed, and she watched him with fascinated wonder. That he should do so to her, plain, puritan Lizzie; that she should love the devil in him. Zek . . .

His smile made her head spin, his body caught fire with hers. Some cold corner of her mind thought—'Making love with one's husband should be done in a dark room beneath the bedclothes. Not . . . not . . . well!

She pictured herself, lying half-naked on the covers, tossing feverishly, Zek still in his shirt, clothing spread from hasty disrobing all about them.

Her long lashes lifted and she looked up into his dark eyes, alive with a hundred emotions, and knew in her heart that he was the only man for her.

Afterwards, when they lay quiet, he said:

'I think it's time we went home.'

'Home?'

'Your home, Lizzie, and mine.'

She shifted uneasily. Angelica.

'What is it?'

She felt him watching her in the half-darkness, and forced herself to say lightly:

'Oh nothing. I was just thinking of facing everyone.'

His laugh was arrogant. 'You're my wife, Lizzie. You needn't make excuses to anybody for your behaviour.'

Somehow she loved him all the more for that.

And so here they were, bumping over the dusty road, on their way 'home'. Her home. Strange, but she had never had a home before. Not a proper, permanent one. She had been shifted and shunted about. She supposed the town house had been a sort of a home, until she was shuffled off to the workhouse. And now she had a real home.

Zek was talking about having some sort of celebration dinner, inviting people from around about so that she could get to know them officially as his wife. It terrified her, thinking of all those mocking faces, but she agreed to it evenly enough, winning an approving smile from her husband.

Jessie Grant was there to welcome her, and whatever she felt was carefully cloaked beneath an attitude of respectful obedience. Mary too seemed more respectful and perhaps even more friendly. The other servants were subdued, and Lizzie, expecting perhaps resentment and dislike, was grateful for that. Ralph Grant smiled at her and congratulated her quite cheerfully, and tried to pretend he had known they were in love from the moment he saw them.

'There's a letter for Mrs Gray,' Jessie said, and it took a moment for Lizzie to realise that was herself.

The letter was from Jane, and she read it avidly, nearly weeping over the spelling errors and the great blot at the end. Dear Jane! She sounded very happy. The tavern was going well, and Johnny was building on to it. She hoped Lizzie had settled in, and was glad to hear from her. How was Mr Gray?

Dear, dear Jane. How Mama would have exclaimed, if she were alive and here now. Jane had always been the beauty, and her mother had hoped one day she would marry well. Lizzie had been expected to do no more than work hard and be respectable. And look how things had turned out. Lizzie had made the brilliant marriage, while Jane . . . but Jane was happy, wasn't she?

Zek had laughed at her excitement over the letter, and listened to her ramblings with a patient look. That annoyed her slightly, but she was too pleased to take him up on it. After dinner, they sat in the cosy sitting-room, and Lizzie hurriedly wrote off to Jane. Zek sipped his brandy, and sat staring into the fire.

'Will you still redecorate the house?' she asked, pausing with pen held over paper.

He glanced at her over his shoulder, where she sat at the desk.

'Of course.'

When she had finished, and was sealing the missive, he said, 'Come here,' in such a gentle voice she could not argue. Smiling, she came, and he snuggled her down beside him on the sofa, his hand smoothing over her wild curls. They sat a moment in silence, and Lizzie thought that if he were to leave her in the morning, she could never have been happier than she was at this moment.

'Ralph tells me Angelica is spreading rumours,' he said softly at last.

She looked up sharply into his eyes, but he was staring into the fire, his face closed.

'She says I married you because her husband suspected we were . . . well, lovers, or some such nonsense, and that I wanted to put his mind at ease so that we could carry on regardless.'

She stiffened, wondering if this was all some sort of cruel game to prepare her for just that eventuality.

'Lizzie? I wanted to tell you in case you heard and . . . well, Angelica once had ambitions in that direction, but it's over. I told her so the night I went to see her. The night you and I . . .'

'I see,' she said, her voice strange and stilted.

His hand stopped smoothing her hair, and he suddenly forced her chin up, staring down at her. His mouth went straight and grim, his black eyes hard and narrow. She gazed back at him, thinking how dangerously handsome he was, and how much she loved him.

'You already believe it, don't you?'

His soft question threw her thoughts into confusion.

'I . . .'

'You do,' he repeated, in a harsh, grating voice, and stood up, swinging around to face her.

'I . . . oh Zek, she's so beautiful!'

'"She's so beautiful"!' he mocked savagely. 'You're a fool, Lizzie, by God you are! Can't you see . . . but no, I suppose *you* can't!'

He flung his glass suddenly and viciously into the fire. The brandy in the bottom burst with a sudden bright flare, while the glass shattered. Lizzie jumped, her eyes wild in her white face.

He was staring into the flames, watching them die a little, his shoulders hunched.

After a moment he turned back to her, his face pale and almost haggard. She thought she saw despair in his eyes, and knew then that he really did love Angelica, and that he was breaking his heart

over her, just as Lizzie was breaking hers over him.
And she couldn't bear it.

With a cry, she jumped up from the sofa and ran
out of the room.

CHAPTER
NINE

SOMEHOW things didn't seem the same after that. Zek worked twice as hard, or so it seemed to Lizzie, and she herself worked in the house and garden. Work commenced on the house, and the constant noise drove her out of it, seeking solace in the orchard. Summer drew on and the wheat had to be harvested and the fruit picked. The place seemed to swell to ten times its normal activity, and extra labour had to be hired and housed and fed. There was plenty to do.

The celebration dinner was shelved—there didn't seem much to celebrate now—and the few visitors Lizzie had were mostly curiosity seekers or friends of Zek who considered he had made a grave error of judgment in marrying Lizzie, or so she thought.

Angelica came riding over, blasé about the whole thing. She smiled a lot at Lizzie, but her blue eyes were mocking and Lizzie knew that the other girl was aware of the truth. Zek had probably already told her, or at least been to reassure her over the matter. She pictured them lying together, and clenched her fists to try and counteract the shaft of pain this caused. Love was supposed to be unselfish, wasn't it? Well then shouldn't she be happy for her husband, if Angelica was what he wanted? If she truly loved him she would be glad, and bear with it all uncomplainingly, a gentle, understanding smile on her mouth day and night. Only it wasn't like that at all! It hurt, and her smile was ragged at the edges, and Zek looked so tired sometimes she wanted to weep.

Sometimes she longed for the days of their honeymoon in Bathurst. They had been happy then; they had! If only they could recapture some of that easy camaraderie. Even the sometimes bitter arguments they had had before their marriage were preferable to this.

He took her into the little town one day, before Christmas. It was very hot that day, a warm wind blistering the earth, and drying her skin, she was sure, like a prune, despite her big hat and sun-shade.

The town was sweltering, and Lizzie was glad to go inside the little shop there, where it was relatively cool. There were sweets in jars, and bags of flour and the like. Everything one could think of. There were even bales of cloth, and Zek confused her by buying a length she had admired. The town had its own hall, and a stone church with a wooden bell tower near the doors.

'Not much perhaps,' he murmured on the way home, 'but it'll grow, Lizzie. They're already talking about a school, and when our kids come along we could send 'em here instead of Bathurst. Unless, of course, you want a tutor.'

She said nothing, wondering bitterly how he thought they would have children when he totally ignored her bed, and she slept alone in the great thing while he slept alone in his own room. She had expected one of them to move, but he had never mentioned it, and she knew now he didn't want her nearer. She supposed, with Angelica to turn to, he would hardly want anything more to do with Lizzie. It was only common sense.

He was watching her. She felt it, and turned her face to meet his stare. Suddenly the wicked light came dancing into his eyes, and he smiled. It was the old smile, the warm, rake's smile.

'Hardly the thoughts of a modest woman, eh, Lizzie?' he murmured, and she realised he had known.

'I don't know what you mean,' she retorted, and glanced away.

But he laughed again. Perhaps that was why he had come to her bed that night. He was absurdly tender, for such a wicked lecher, and when she woke in the morning he was smiling at her in the old, possessive way, the light from the shutters slanting across his cheekbones.

He took her wrist in his fingers, brushing his thumb back and forth, his eyes on hers. 'I can feel your pulse,' he said, smiling. 'I can feel you living and breathing and being.'

His mouth went straight, and his body tensed. She watched, a little puzzled, as he bent his head so that the shadows hid his expression from her.

'It's always fascinated me, to feel a person living like that, and to know that that little beat could stop so suddenly, for whatever reason. Fascinating, and terrifying.'

'Zek, don't,' she whispered.

'Sorry.' He laughed, an oddly strained sound, and bent to kiss her rather bruisingly on the mouth before climbing out of the bed.

She watched him stretching, the muscles of his back rippling with the movement, before moving to the door, completely unconcerned with his nakedness. He was a beautiful man, strong and sleek and brown from the sun. She let her eyes drink in his beauty, as he turned to smile at her.

'If you look at me like that, Lizzie-mine, I won't be doing any work today,' he mocked, and she blushed and turned away. His soft laughter lingered long after he had closed the door.

Angelica invited them to a party some weeks after. She came over to issue the invitation herself, and Lizzie privately thought it about time she did so. Christmas was only days away, and Christmas should be a time of kindness and happiness. Not that she could expect much of either from Angelica.

'Zek always comes to my parties,' the girl said, with a laugh.

'So he said.'

'I'm sure you'll enjoy it! Do come with him.'

As if she would let him go alone! She was certain though that she wouldn't enjoy it. Zek seemed pleased she was going, however, and she made an effort to appear at her poor best. Any best would be poor alongside Angelica.

Lizzie put on her blue silk, that Zek had admired so, and put up her hair so that it fluffed out softly about her sharp features, adding some of the jewels that Zek had bought her to her ears and throat.

He smiled when he saw her, and kissed her cheek. 'You smell all clean and fresh,' he said, his arms about her shoulders. His fingers squeezed. 'You had a letter from that sister of yours, I believe.'

'Yes.' She frowned. 'She wished us happy but . . . she sounded so odd. As though she were worrying about something. I don't know. I wish I could talk to her face to face; I'd soon drag it out of her!'

'Invite her to stay.'

'I will, but I know she won't come. They're too busy with the building and everything.'

'Maybe she thinks I ill-treat you,' he said, in a quiet voice.

She glanced at him, knowing the white look would be tensing his jaw. When she didn't reply, his mouth hardened even more.

'Come on, we'd best get going to the Baileys'.'

She came willingly enough, but beneath the expensive gown her heart was aching. He was thinking of Angelica, and how much more he'd rather be married to her.

Lizzie had not been to the Baileys' place before.

She found it almost as large as Zek's house, though not so well-run and tidy looking, if she did say so herself! The house was all lit up, and the gardens had been cunningly filled with coloured lanterns. Angelica came to meet them, resplendent in a gown of pink and mauve, cut so low Lizzie felt sure she would fall right out of it. Her eyes shone like sapphires, and she laughed rather a lot, showing her pointed white teeth.

There were others there, all patronising, taking their cue from their hostess, Lizzie thought wryly. Mr Bailey was not as old as she had been led to believe. In his late forties, perhaps, though illness had aged him and his wrists were like sticks coming from the cuffs of his shirt.

She felt sorry for him—after all, their situations were of a muchness—and sat with him after the meal, talking about her voyage from London. He laughed at her jokes, and his eyes were warm and grateful, a little like a dog which has been ill-treated and now finds itself with a kinder master. But his gaze, every now and again, slid away to where Angelica stood, fascinating her little audience. She was as beautiful as a star, and her husband obviously still loved her despite what she had done to him.

'She's very lovely, isn't she?' he asked Lizzie. He turned, meeting her eyes eagerly, hands gripping the rests of his chair a little nervously. 'I married her in Sydney Town, you know. I was not so . . . helpless then. She was on the stage there. Came in from London and took the town by storm. I fell in love with her, and she with me. Of course, it was different, with me able to get out of this acursed chair in those days. I matched her, dare for dare. Now . . .' his hands went limp, and he stared down at the floor, suddenly old and worn out.

'She is very lovely,' Lizzie murmured gently.

He made no motion that he had heard her. Had Angelica loved him? Or had she loved the thought of his money and his cloak of respectability and being mistress of her own home and servants? Perhaps she had loved him, when he was able to match her. But now he was confined to an invalid's chair, Angelica felt herself free to look elsewhere. He must realise that. He was obviously not a fool.

'Mrs Gray.'

She looked up into the bright blue eyes in the worn, pain-creased features. 'Mr Bailey? I'm sorry, I was far away.'

He returned her smile. 'I haven't congratulated you on your marriage. I must admit it was quite a surprise to me when Zek Gray rushed you off to Bathurst and put his ring on your finger. But now that I've met you I can understand why he shouldn't want anyone else snapping you up.'

He meant it, and Lizzie laughed naturally.

His smile faded, and a crease joined the others on his brow. 'He is not an easy man to understand, Mrs Gray. And not an easy man, I should think, to hold. That you have done so is rather remarkable.'

'You mean he is . . . was rather a rake,' she retorted, and rather shocked herself by her plain-speaking.

But he shrugged. 'Perhaps I do, perhaps I do. He must be in his mid-thirties, and no man reaches that age without some experience behind him, Mrs Gray. You can't hold that against a man. I remember myself . . .' But his smile twisted with bitter-ness. 'Never mind that. Don't want to shock you.'

She laughed. 'I'm beginning to think I don't shock as easily as I once did, Mr Bailey.'

He reached out as if to pat her hand, changed his mind and fell silent.

He was thinking of Angelica and Zek. Had they succeeded in putting him off the scent with this marriage? He seemed to imagine Zek had married her for love. It made Lizzie feel dirty, deceiving him in that way, but to tell him the truth would be worse.

Her eyes searched the crowded room and found Zek. He was drinking again; he had been drinking all evening. She had tried to catch his eye once, but he turned his back on her and began flirting with a girl with red hair. Lizzie gave up. When she noticed him again he was watching her, eyes narrowed across the distance. 'See,' he seemed to be saying, 'I can have any woman in this room, Lizzie. What do you think of that?' The thought hurt her, but she bore it grimly.

'Lizzie?'

She looked up. He was standing by Bailey's

chair, his face pale, his eyes gleaming. Bailey also looked up, his expression hardening at the sight of Zek. Dislike stiffened every line of him, and seeing that, Zek smiled. A mocking, cynical smile that caused Lizzie to draw a sharp breath.

'Zek,' she said, and stood up, taking his arm firmly in hers.

'Gray,' Bailey muttered, and looked away.

Zek moved as if to confront him again, but Lizzie pulled on his arm, drawing him away. He looked down into her face, an eyebrow lifting with amusement.

'Are you afraid I'll hit him, Lizzie?' he said conversationally.

'No. But as he dislikes you I thought it best if you left him alone.'

His face darkened; she felt the muscles of his arm go hard as iron.

'I'm sick and tired of him looking through me. If he has something to say to me, why doesn't he say it?'

'Zek,' she whispered, as his voice rose. Some people turned to stare. 'Zek, please, it doesn't matter what he thinks.'

'And what about you, Lizzie? What do you think?'

The dark eyes were fastened on her face, and she couldn't hide the dismay and fear and sick knowledge that passed over it. He stood a moment more, gazing into her eyes, and then he had wrenched his arm out of her slackened grip, and was striding towards Angelica. Lizzie watched him break into the circle, watched the woman's suddenly brilliant smile, the way she leaned against him, touching. Always touching. When she could bear no more, Lizzie turned away. When she steeled herself to

look again, some time later, the couple were no-
where to be found.

For a moment she felt as if she'd suddenly fallen
from high above. A sensation of headlong flight,
spinning dizziness, and the agony of striking earth.
Her head ached, and she fought her pain grimly,
telling herself it was no more than she had known
all along.

'Mrs Gray?'

Kind blue eyes. A plump, dark haired woman.
They had been introduced before. Edna Tucker?
Yes, that was it. She had apologised for not calling
on Lizzie, only her youngest child had been very
ill.

Lizzie managed to summon up a smile.

Mrs Tucker said gently, 'It's rather stuffy in here.
Are you feeling the heat, my dear? Perhaps you'd
like some fresh air.'

'Yes, thank you. Perhaps I shall go outside.'

The windows into the garden were open, and
Lizzie and Edna Tucker walked out into the cool
foliage. Crickets sang, and moths hovered about
the lanterns. Edna was chatting about the summer
harvest, and how lucky they had been with the rain
coming just when it should, and how lucky they
were that it had come at all.

'I've known it to be so dry the ground cracks and
scorches, and even our river dries up.'

'How terrible,' Lizzie whispered, her brown eyes
huge.

The other woman smiled, taking Lizzie's arm in
hers as they strolled.

'You mustn't mind Angelica,' she said at last.
'She must have every man in love with her! It's her
way.'

So Edna Tucker had seen what happened. Lizzie

supposed everyone else in the room had seen it also. More gossip, more pain.

'I shouldn't think it would be too difficult,' she said. 'With Angelica's looks.'

Edna looked at her a moment. 'Forgive me, Mrs Gray, but . . . looks are not so important. It's what's inside that counts.'

Lizzie glanced up at her, and saw suddenly that her face had gone rigid, and she was dragging Lizzie's arm, trying to pull her away.

'My dear, I think you'd better go back.'

Lizzie, startled, naturally turned to see what had frightened Edna so, because Mrs Tucker did look frightened. So she turned, brown eyes huge, and her body went to ice. Or so it seemed at the moment. Because there, hardly even attempting to hide themselves behind the branches of a pepper-corn tree, were Angelica and Zek.

They were embracing, so tightly they might have been one, and Zek was kissing her savagely. Somehow Lizzie found herself turned to the house, staring at the lighted windows of the rooms. Edna had her arm about her shoulders and was holding the shivering girl against her. 'Never mind, never mind,' she was murmuring, leading her gently back the way they had come. Lizzie heard Angelica's laughter behind them, smothered abruptly by Zek's mouth.

It was as if something inside her really did break then, because she began to retch, and Edna held her head while she was violently ill in one of Angelica's untidy flower borders.

The other woman was extremely kind, Lizzie thought afterwards, to someone she hardly knew. She led Lizzie into a small, empty parlour, and sat her down, bringing her some brandy to warm her, and put some colour back into her stark cheeks. Gradually Lizzie stopped shivering and shaking, and even managed a smile.

'That's better,' Edna said, patting her hand. 'And never mind, my dear. It never lasts, you know. Angelica can never stay with one man for more than a month. I know that, Mrs Gray, because even my poor dear husband was not immune.'

Lizzie's brown eyes shone with compassion. 'I'm so sorry!'

But Edna Tucker smiled. 'It didn't last. He saw her for what she was, I hope, and she grew bored. We pretend it never happened, which is why we feel we must come when she invites us. To pretend.'

Lizzie sighed. 'But it's different with Zek,' she whispered. 'She wants him, she always has. All of them want him. And he loves her. That's the awful part. He loves her, and if she hadn't been married already I wouldn't be here now.'

Edna shook her head, blue eyes helpless in her compassion. Lizzie, seeing how upset the other woman was, dried her eyes and took a deep breath.

'I'm all right now. Really! I'll just rest here for a moment. It was just the . . . the shock of seeing something I already knew confirmed.'

'Are you quite sure, Mrs Gray?'

'Yes. And thank you so much.'

But Edna just smiled, and closed the door softly after her.

Lizzie sat staring at it, feeling ill and weak and shaky. Zek and Angelica. Well, she had feared it . . . known it, in a way. Zek loved her, and if Lizzie loved Zek she must let him go without making things worse. The fact that Angelica was selfish and wicked mustn't make any difference. It was Zek she must think of. Zek, whom she loved.

But that only started the tears again, and she sighed, drying her cheeks. She took another sip of the brandy, and took another deep breath. Perhaps, as Edna said, it wouldn't last. Although it had lasted this long. Was she allowed no hope to cling to? No promises, no matter how false they were?

After a moment she stood up, patting her clothes into place and smoothing her hair in the mirror over the fireplace. She was about to return to the others when the door opened and Zek looked in. He saw her, and frowning, came striding towards her, his hands outstretched.

'Edna Tucker said you were feeling unwell. Lizzie?'

She backed away from him, knowing it was too soon and she couldn't face him naturally after what she had just seen. He saw something of the misery and anger on her face and stopped dead in his tracks.

'Lizzie?'

But he knew. She watched the colour stain his brown cheeks.

'You saw us, didn't you? Angelica laughed and said that you had, but I . . . it's not what you think, Lizzie-mine.' But his voice had a grim desperation to it, as though he were fighting a lost battle.

'Zek, please—'

'You know what she's like, Lizzie. It meant nothing. I did it because you seemed to expect me to, and I . . .'

'I really don't care,' she whispered. This, she decided, was the best way to handle it. Make him think it didn't matter to her, that there was no need to explain. Only don't let him lie, and go on lying.

He laughed shakily. 'No, I don't suppose you do. I'd forgotten that. But you've never pretended to love me, have you, wife-of-mine?'

'Zek . . .'

'Well, it's hardly surprising, is it? It was a marriage of convenience for both of us, wasn't it? Nothing like your sister's blissful union, hmm?'

His savage sarcasm rocked her. She felt so dizzy suddenly she clung to the mantelpiece.

'Angelica seems to love me, Lizzie. In her way, she's been true to me. It can't be much of a life for her, tied to a living-dead man, can it? And she's so beautiful, as you said yourself.'

The room was tilting, as if she were drunk, only this time she wasn't. She felt the nausea clutching at her stomach, and tried to hold it back. Perspiration began to show on her face, making it shine. If only he would go away, she could be ill in peace.

'Don't do this to me, Zek,' she whispered, but he didn't hear.

'Like an angel herself, eh, Lizzie? She rides like the wind, too, which isn't something you're terribly good at, is it? And she doesn't mind showing a man what she thinks of him, one way and another . . . Lizzie?'

But Lizzie had leaned her forehead against the marble of the fireplace, biting her lip. Her sickness could no longer be hidden or denied. Zek was holding her, though she hardly knew it now, even when he kissed her brow, rocking her against him as if he alone could cure her.

'Take me home,' she breathed, and had fainted away even before he had swung her up into his strong arms.

She recalled, vaguely, being lifted into her seat,

and the jolt of the journey home. The lights dazzled
her when they arrived there, and faces hovered,
like ghosts. Someone undressed her and put her
into bed, bathing her face and soothing her, while
she was ill in a convenient basin. She was ill again
later on, but after that felt much better. Only so
weak and wretched.

Morning found her feeling rather better, and she
rose carefully, and threw open the shutters, breathing the cool fresh morning air. The world was
waking, the sky was blue, and she smiled until she
remembered Angelica. Her smile gave way to sad-
ness, and she dressed slowly, determined to tell
Zek finally that she understood, that he needn't
feel guilty. That, as he loved Angelica so much it
was making him into a different man, Lizzie would
make no demur at their resumed affair.

But when she came into the dining-room and he
looked up, so surprised to see her, all such unselfish
thoughts left her mind. He looked absolutely haggard, his skin had a greyish tint, and by the look of
him he hadn't slept all night. If that was what love
did to one, Lizzie thought shakily, it seemed hardly
worth falling into.

'Lizzie!' He started up, finding his voice at last.

She sat down with the faintest of smiles, and
glanced over the breakfast trays.

'Good morning.'

A jab of hunger set her busying herself with her
plate. She was absolutely ravenous!

'But . . . are you all right?' Zek whispered,
though more moderately.

'Well I think so,' and she forced another smile, as
hunger gnawed at her stomach.

His black eyes mocked her sudden greed. They
ate in silence, though she did most of the eating.

Zek sat and watched her, a smile playing about his mouth, his face creased in thought. She wondered if she should mention Angelica now, but they seemed so companionable it seemed a pity to spoil the mood. She would tell him later . . . tonight. Yes, tonight was soon enough.

Mary too seemed surprised to see her up, but pleased when Lizzie smiled at her worried clucking.

'I think it must have been something I ate at Mrs Bailey's which disagreed,' she told the girl.

'But you were quite feverish, ma'am!' Mary said reprovingly. 'Mr Gray remarked on it particularly. Didn't you, sir?'

Zek rose abruptly, startling them into looking at him. 'Yes,' he said quietly. He paused by her chair. 'Take special care today, Lizzie. I don't want my wife falling ill, whatever you may think of my morals.'

Did he not? Wouldn't that solve all their problems? Her meal tasted suddenly of sawdust, and she pushed her plate aside.

'He was very worried, ma'am,' Mary murmured beside her. 'I never seen Mr Gray that worried before in all my time here. He must love you very much.'

Guilt, Lizzie thought. Guilt had made him distraught, when he believed his scene with Angelica had caused her sudden illness. Now she was better again he could go back to that cat with a clear conscience.

But it was not so. Lizzie was ill again almost immediately, and lay on her bed, certain nothing could ever make her feel any worse. The room was stuffy and hot, despite the open shutters, and in the afternoon she made the effort to get up and make her way slowly out into the garden. But the exertion proved too much and she fainted. After that, Zek insisted she remain in her bed, and when he caught her trying to get up he was so furious and white-faced she was too afraid to do anything other than obey him.

'I'm taking you into Bathurst to see a doctor, my girl,' he told her, 'and let's hear no more of it.'

She was feeling so wretched she didn't argue, which was itself an oddity, but lay listless, watching him pace the room.

'We'll see what he says,' he was saying, more to himself than her. 'I'm not a pauper, Lizzie, and I . . .'

But whatever it was he had been about to say was interrupted. Mary came in, murmuring that Edna Tucker was here with her husband to visit.

Zek nodded, and went out. A few minutes later Edna appeared in the doorway, blue eyes worried.

'Lizzie . . . Mrs Gray! I'm so sorry to see you still in bed.'

Lizzie smiled wryly. 'So am I.'

Edna came and sat by her, chatting gently about her children. After a time they fell silent, and Lizzie, watching the other woman, knew she was gathering courage to speak of last night.

'Lizzie . . . I'm sure you're quite wrong when you say your husband and Angelica are . . . well. I've seen how worried he is about you, and—'

'He seems worried, yes,' Lizzie murmured. 'And I'm sorry for that, because Zek has enough on his mind without me being such a fool.'

Edna patted her hand gently.

They stayed for dinner, and Lizzie was sorry she could not join them. But Zek expressly forbade it. However, she was feeling so well some hours later that she decided to dress and make an appearance.

I'll surprise them all, she thought, smiling as she smoothed her hair. And with those people there, Zek can't abuse me too much, can he?

She thought a breath of fresh air might do her good, so she went out on to the verandah via the side door, walking quietly and slowly around past the dining-room window. It was in darkness, but the sitting-room one wasn't, and she hesitated nearby, hearing voices. At last she took a deep breath and moved towards it, intending to peep in and see who was there before she made her entrance. If only Zek was in a better mood, she thought, as she moved.

'So you see,' Zek was saying, 'I don't know what to say to her. She obviously doesn't know of it or . . . but maybe she does, maybe she just doesn't want to think about it . . .'

'I can't believe it,' Edna murmured. 'A fever. A . . . an illness is not necessarily a fatal one!'

'Oh yes, I told myself that at first. But it's happening! She's getting more and more attacks, and they're getting worse. How can I not believe she's going to die?'

'Mr Gray!'

He turned from where he was standing in front of the fireplace, and Lizzie caught her breath. He was as white as his shirt, his face drawn with some strain she could only guess at. Edna rose, taking his arm, and Lizzie saw that she also was white-faced. Of Mr Tucker there was no sign, and she could only suppose him to be elsewhere about the house.

'I thought it might be last night,' he went on, as if Edna hadn't spoken, and turned his back again, resting his hands on the mantel. 'But this morning she seemed so much better. It didn't last though. All day long it's been the same. Better, worse, better . . . I won't give up though; I'll take her to the doctor and maybe he'll be able to treat her.'

The soft voice faltered. Lizzie saw his shoulders stiffen. When he looked around he was perfectly white, and for a moment Lizzie thought he was going to collapse. Edna made a movement, but he recovered, gripping the mantelpiece, his knuckles shaking with the strain.

'The thing is,' he said in an oddly dead voice, 'she's dying in front of my eyes, Edna.'

'Zek, I'm sure . . . Zek!'

But he was shaking his head, his black eyes tormented. 'I'm going to have to stop and watch it,' he said. 'I owe it to her, and . . . God give me strength, Edna, to bear that final burden!'

Lizzie spun back against the wall, as white-faced as they. Slowly the truth seemed to dawn on her. They had been speaking of her, Lizzie Gray. And she was dying. She really was dying. There was no way in which she could disbelieve the passionate sound of Zek's voice, his face . . . She was dying and he knew it and the thought of what was to come, her getting weaker and more dependent, clinging to him when he didn't love her, was a source of horror to him. Oh God, she thought, please no! She would be another Mr Bailey.

The thought sickened her.

She bit her knuckles to stop the sudden scream.

The darkness mocked her, a cool breeze curling her hair about her white face, cooling her hot cheeks, stirring her skirts. Oh Jane, where are you when I need you? Oh Zek . . . She opened her eyes again, and stared blindly down over the dark road to Bathurst, remembering Thomas Bailey's eyes, following Angelica about, and his lined, pain-creased face.

There was only really one way for Lizzie to take. She would go with Zek to see the doctor he secretly knew would be unable to help her, and somehow contrive to slip away from them. Jane would take her in and care for her, until it was over. She would no longer be a burden to Zek then, and . . . But it was all too much suddenly to take in, and the tears returned, running silently down her cheeks.

CHAPTER
TEN

SURPRISINGLY, she slept deeply, and woke refreshed and further determined to carry through her plan. She no longer pretended to herself that she was better. She would never be better again. She would have another attack, and then another, until she died.

She took a deep breath and tried to think clearly. The fact was she was dying, impossible though such a thing seemed, and Zek was to be burdened with her ailing body. Did she want that? Lying in her bed, pathetically awaiting his visits. His kind smile, compassion, the weight of her like a ball and chain about his neck. No! No, she did not want such a thing to happen.

Last night she had thought of Jane as an escape. This morning she thought of Jane again, and knew it was the only way out. Jane loved her, and would shield her. She would be glad to die, if Jane was with her, and Zek was happy with Angelica.

A light breakfast on a tray didn't bring about a return of the awful retching, or the dizzy spells. She rested quietly until she was certain she was all right, then she went out to find Zek.

He was in his office. She had thought, after what she had witnessed last night, that he would be unable to face her. But when he looked up at her 'good morning' his smile seemed genuine. A little strained about the edges, perhaps, as her own was, but then if she hadn't known differently she would have assumed that was because of Angelica.

'Lizzie, how are you?'

'A little better I think,' she replied quietly.

'In that case I think we'd better get in to Bathurst as soon as possible. Can you get Mary to pack some things for you?'

'Yes, of course.'

He looked down at the letter he had been writing, staring at it as if he didn't recognise the words. After a moment he said, 'Good. We'll go as soon as you're ready.'

She went out on to the verandah, watching life go on about her as if she were already dead, and a ghost at the proceedings. She was numb with the shock of it all, and didn't try very hard to shake it off. Better to be numb until she got to Jane, and then . . . then she could begin to feel again.

Mary packed while she sat and watched her. The girl seemed heavy-eyed, but friendly enough, and chattered to Lizzie. Zek, it seemed had ridden off to the Baileys' place for a short visit, and Lizzie didn't even allow herself to imagine what might be said between him and Angelica. He was back an hour later, looking unimaginably tired, which only swelled her determination to remove the burden of herself from his shoulders.

His light affection was the hardest thing to bear. He treated her tenderly even, his black eyes warm and gentle. It made her want to throw herself into his arms and cling to him, begging to be allowed to stay. But how could she? He would keep her, because he was kind, but he would suffer twice the cost if he knew she loved him. Poor Zek. And poor Lizzie.

She remembered now his watchful looks. Had he

known, even then, how it would be? How had he known? It made no sense, but then to die made little sense either. It was best not to think . . . but despite herself she remembered how he had felt her pulse and said those things about it stopping. The tears would start if she kept this up, she told herself angrily, and concentrated instead on Jane.

She had saved money from her housekeeper days, and put this in the small bag with her change of clothing and a warm cloak. They would not need more, Zek had said, because after she had seen the doctor he would be bringing her back home. To die, she thought miserably. Only it would be Zek alone who came back . . . to Angelica.

They started out around mid-morning. Lizzie felt a little faint at first, but Zek ensured her comfort and tucked a rug solicitously about her knees until the sun grew too hot. He seemed talkative, but she thought it cost him an effort. He was watchful too, and she pretended not to notice.

They rested along the way again, and reached Bathurst in the evening. Zek sent her up to rest again before dinner. She told him she wanted to go shopping in the morning, and he let her run on, smiling faintly, though the lines in his face seemed deeper than ever.

He drew the curtains for her, and covered her with a quilt, smoothing back her curls from her brow. 'I'll be back soon then, Lizzie,' he whispered, and stooping kissed her temple.

When he had gone she shed tears into her pillow, stifling her sobs as best she could. Why couldn't he be brutal? Then she might possibly be able to hate him. Instead of which her love grew and grew.

Lizzie woke the following morning feeling quite strong. Zek had already gone out to make an appointment with the doctor, who had been out on an emergency the night before. Lizzie slipped out to find a means of transport to Jane. There was no regular coach service to and from Sydney Town, but she found a merchant's office, and he seemed willing to take her aboard his wagon for a fee. This was agreed upon, and she returned to the hotel for her bag.

She had climbed the stairs and was reaching for the door knob when she heard the voices. The thought passed through Lizzie's mind that she seemed to spend much of her time lately eavesdropping. And she didn't consciously mean to do so this time, but as she hesitated at the door the overheard conversation sank into her mind.

'I don't know what to think,' Zek said, and his voice was bitter. 'She seems to have withdrawn into herself. She doesn't need me at all!'

'Zek, I'm sorry.'

'I may as well not be there.' Footsteps pacing the floor. 'Leigh, what can I do?'

'Damn it, Zek! What can *I* say? It seems bloody unfair to me!'

Unfair, that he was hampered with an ailing wife, when Angelica was waiting. Captain Barrett obviously recognised the injustice of this as much as Zek, and Lizzie bit her lip with sudden self-pity.

'I'm in a hell of a situation,' Zek muttered. 'I feel like I'm being torn in two!'

'Old man, here, here. Look, come and let me buy you a drink. We'll try and sort something out. Kitten might be able to help, you know. Kitten's very good with problems.'

'God, I just haven't the heart for it, Leigh . . .'

Lizzie flattened herself behind the rather ugly

grandfather clock in the passageway, when they came out. They went past her, heads close together, without even noticing her. She let out a deep breath, watching them pass down the stairs and into the entrance hall. Mrs O'Driscoll trapped them there, her hands waving with animated conversation. After a moment more they got by her, Leigh patted Zek on the back as they went out into the street. Mrs O'Driscoll went back into her little room behind the desk.

It took but a moment for Lizzie to get her bag. It took another minute to pen a note to Zek. It was brief and brusque—She would be all right. She was leaving him. She did not wish to see him again, ever. She appreciated all he had done for her, but she did not love him nor want him to come for her or contact her. It was over.

The black ink on white paper was uncompromising, even harsh, but she knew it was the only way. Guilt and worry for her safety might make him pursue her. This blow to his pride and the relief of knowing she did not love him would stop him. She had freed him, and at the same time destroyed any hope she had of happiness.

Lizzie was out into the street before she knew it, light-headed, but whether from her illness or the fact of her escape she did not know or care. An hour later, she was aboard the wagon, rumbling on her way back to Jane.

The journey over the mountains was slow, tedious, and in parts terrifying. The wagon groaned up the slopes and rocked down winding declines. It began to rain half-way over, and the sludge made the wheels slide and slip, while the driver cursed and laid into his horses with his whip.

Lizzie, clinging to the seat beside him, felt ill and cold, and almost wished she had never left, despite all she had overheard. Oh Zek, she thought, and lifted her face so that her tears could mingle with the rain. He would have looked after her, been her strength, her crutch. And, a cold voice whispered, he would have hated you for it.

They made camp after they had passed over the mountains, and Lizzie was given a share in the man's food. He was about forty, with sharp eyes and a wiry strength. She thought, if she had been pretty and a bit more lively, he might have offered to share his blanket with her. As it was, she curled up in her cloak under the wagon, cramped and cold, but unmolested.

They set out again as the sun rose, and made their long way on towards Sydney Town. The miles dragged, and Lizzie slumped in her seat, no longer feeling the bumps and rattles, or the pains in her bones. Her head ached dully, but other than that she felt well.

Evanstown went by at last, and then there it was. The Thirsty Felon. Lizzie had never imagined she would be so glad to see it, and she hardly paused to thank the taciturn driver before she was off, running on light feet towards the open door.

Johnny looked up, his face startled, and then suddenly it broke into a wide grin. He came hurrying up to her.

'Lizzie! You've come visiting at last! Where's your man?'

Lizzie burst into tears.

Johnny paused, and then wrapped his arms about her. There was something incredibly soothing about being in his arms, and she wept out all her terrors and hurts.

'Jane!' he called, still holding her. 'Jane love!'

Jane came with a rustle of skirts, flushed and panting. 'I was out at the barn and . . . Lizzie!'

Jane's plump bosom was even more comforting than being held by Johnny, and Lizzie held her sister to her as if she would never let her go. Jane led her to a chair and sat her down, fetching water and a handkerchief.

'Lizzie, Lizzie! What is it . . . Zek isn't . . . Oh Lizzie, he ain't dead!'

Lizzie shook her head, snuffling and wiping her face. After a moment she took a long breath and looked up at the two expectant, worried faces— Jane all flushed and glowing, Johnny pale and pleasantly ugly.

'I've left him,' she said huskily.

Jane moved impatiently. 'I can see that, Liz. Why?'

Lizzie bit her lip.

'Come on Lizzie,' Jane said sharply. 'What's he done?'

Something in her sister's eyes stilled Lizzie's tongue. Jane looked absolutely riddled with guilt. Lizzie remembered the letter that had puzzled her so with its vague hints and worries. Jane, seeing her sister knit her brow, sighed.

'Yes, it's time we both had a bit of a talk, Liz. Come on. Johnny can clean up in here while we go and have a quiet chat in the back room.

The back room was new to Lizzie, and quite cosy, though somewhat jumbled with furniture. Lizzie found a space and sat down, eyeing Jane's flushed face. Her sister looked plumper than before, more matronly somehow. But it suited her, and she seemed happy. Which was more than could be said for Lizzie.

'He loves someone else,' she said tragically. 'He only married me because she was already married, and her husband suspected something between them. He was going to carry on as before, except that . . .' she twisted the handkerchief between her fingers, wondering how to break the news gently to her sister, who was leaning forward with a rapt expression. 'I'm sick, Jane,' she whispered, gulping back more tears. 'I overheard him and . . . oh Jane, he's sorry for me and is tearing himself in two over me and this other woman. So I've left him. I can't bear him to pity me, Jane. He's so miserable about it all and . . . I just couldn't!'

'Hush now . . .'

Jane took her sister into her arms, rocking her until the sobs quietened. Lizzie broke away, wiping her eyes with a shaking hand. It was only then she realised how quiet Jane had become. She looked up, and saw that her sister was biting her lips, dismay mingling with . . . yes, her eyes were alight with humour!

'Jane,' she whispered.

'Oh Lizzie . . . Lizzie, I've something to confess. Something I'm not at all proud of. Johnny's told me I was a fool, and so I am. Only I meant it for the best, and I beg you to remember that, when I'm done.'

The blue eyes searched hers pleadingly, then she stared down at her hands. 'Do you remember when Zek Gray arrived for the wedding, Lizzie? Well I had it all planned, you see. I had seen him kiss you, when you were ill here that time, and how gentle he was with you, when you was sick. He seems to be a man who shows gentleness to sick and ailing folk. I thought . . . well, I thought you were more fond of him than you'd let on.'

Lizzie was beginning to frown, and Jane hurried on before she lost courage.

'I thought, in time . . . oh, it was stupid, Lizzie! A childish thing to do. I never thought of the consequences. Well . . . the truth now. I told Zek that day that you was ill, Lizzie. Much more ill than you realised. I only meant to say you was . . . delicate-like, but somehow me tongue ran away with me—you know what I'm like at telling fibs, love—and before I knew what I was about I'd told him you had a fatal illness.'

'A fatal—' Lizzie whispered, her mouth dropping open. Oh God, it was beginning to make a terrible sense to her.

'Yes,' Jane said grimly. 'I said that you would keep getting bad attacks like . . . like the fever you had here, though you'd be perfectly well in between. I said . . . I said the attacks'd get more and more frequent though, and worse and worse and . . . you'd die.'

'Jane!'

'Oh Lizzie, I'm that sorry. I don't think he really believed me though, not at first. I saw him watching you later, and maybe he thought it was a joke or something. I hoped though, Lizzie, if he was worried for you he might be kinder to you and . . . you loved him, didn't you?'

Lizzie nodded. 'I think I must have all along. I kept telling myself how bad he was and . . . you remember, Jane, what I thought of him? And all the time I was saying those things, I loved him.'

'I wanted your happiness, Lizzie. I thought he'd be kinder to you and maybe you'd make a go of it. I thought he'd soon forget my story anway, when he saw that you didn't get ill again and everything was all right. Only . . . Though I kept telling myself I'd

explain it to you both years from now and we'd all
have a good laugh, it began to worry me more and
more, and . . . no one is laughing, Lizzie.'

'Oh Jane, Jane, how could you,' Lizzie breathed.
'I really thought I was dying! He did, too. Jane!'
She turned with huge brown eyes. 'If I'm not . . . if
it was all a story . . . what's wrong with me then,
I've been ever so sick, Jane! Jane!'

'Hush now, Lizzie, calm down. What's it like
then, this sickness?'

Jane's brow puckered, as Lizzie started to explain, in a halting, frightened voice. Gradually,
however, the frown vanished, and Jane's lips
curved up.

'Oh Lizzie,' she cried, giving a peal of laughter, 'I
know what it must be. You're such an innocent!'

'What is it? Jane, please . . .'

'You're going to have a baby. That's all.'

That was all. Lizzie tried to speak, couldn't, tried
again. It came out as a croak. 'A what?'

'A baby,' Jane repeated more gently, and hugged her sister so tightly she could hardly breathe.
'You're going to be a mother. Oh Lord, who'd
believe it? You, a mother,' and she went off into
more peals of laughter.

It took some time for Lizzie to grasp the importance of the fact, and to realise that Jane was
probably right. And when she did believe it, she
began to weep again with a mixture of joy and
despair.

'You love him very much, don't you Lizzie,' Jane
murmured, watching her sister's ineffectual
attempts to stem the tide. 'You'd have to, to leave
him so's he could get back to another woman. And
when you really needed him so much for yourself.
Oh Liz, are you sure he—'

Lizzie blew her nose determinedly. 'Never mind, Jane. The baby doesn't really make a difference. He'd still feel he had to stay with me, and I'd be a burden to him, and . . . I couldn't do that to him. Not to Zek. I saw his face, Jane, when he knew the burden I was going to be, and how I was going to keep him from the woman he really loves, and I never want to see him look like that again. As though he were being slowly drained of life and blood. Jane.' She drew a shaky breath. 'Do you think I can stay here a little while, until I'm sorted out?'

'As long as you like,' Jane said promptly. And then, with a gleam in her eyes, 'You'll never guess who passed through here last month, my girl! One of your admirers.'

Lizzie looked blank, and Jane sighed.

'Jason Wilson, Lizzie! From the voyage over. He's in Sydney. He even left me an address, so's I could call on him any time I'm down there. You too, I expect. I told him about you and Mr Gray, Liz, but by the look of him I'd say he weren't too pleased.'

'Oh. It seems so long ago . . . I mean, the voyage and all.'

A pause, and then Jane rested her hand on Lizzie's, her manner and tone soft and contrite. 'I've done a stupid and cruel thing to you. Can you ever forgive me, Lizzie?'

Lizzie smiled. 'I think so, my dear. Without you saying what you did he might never have offered me the position of housekeeper, and certainly wouldn't have married me.'

'But without me saying it, you wouldn't be here now, crying your eyes out,' Jane muttered, brooding.

Lizzie sighed. 'It's done, Jane, and no amount of regrets will undo it.'

After a moment Jane said, 'You'll have the baby, Liz, whatever happens.'

The baby. Zek's and hers. Lizzie smiled at the idea of it, wondering how she could ever have thought she was dying. It seemed so ridiculous now, so stupid. All that fuss!

Johnny appeared in the doorway. 'Jane, there's customers.'

Jane rose, smoothing her skirts, and went out into the tap-room. Johnny lingered, eyeing Lizzie.

'You look tired. Rest up, Lizzie. We can have a talk later.'

She nodded, and found a bed in the old room she and Jane had occupied when they first arrived. It was done out quite nicely now, with curtains and a counterpane and a proper bed for two. She lay down, listening to the murmur of voices through the door that led into the tap-room, and was almost instantly asleep.

Dreams woke her some hours later, and she lay staring into the darkness thinking of Zek and the baby, and listening to Jane and Johnny talking softly next door. After a moment she rose with an effort and went to find them.

Jane looked up with a smile, and Johnny poured Liz a cup of tea from the pot they had on the fire. She sipped it, smiling gratefully and cupping it in her cold hands.

'It's like old times,' Johnny said, summoning a wink. Lizzie smiled, and Jane nudged him with her elbow.

Johnny stoked the fire and said, 'Do you want to send word to him, Lizzie? He's probably guessed you're here anyway, but it might set his mind at rest, if he knew certain-like.'

She shook her head. 'Knowing I've gone's more likely to set him at rest! If I tell him where I am he might think he has to come and fetch me home like a dutiful husband.'

There was a silence, Jane bit her lip and looked miserable. Lizzie reached out and patted her hand. 'It's not your fault, love!' she said gently. 'What's done is done.'

Johnny nodded. 'I've told her that, but she seems to enjoy being a martyr and miserable. Maybe we should agree with her that it is all her fault and she'd be happy.'

Jane elbowed him again, but her eyes were loving as they met his. Lizzie looked away, suddenly feeling empty as an oyster shell that's been picked clean and left to dry on the beach.

'There's plenty of things to do around here, if you want to stay and help,' Jane went on. Then, to Johnny, 'Liz here is going to have a baby!'

He laughed, turning to Lizzie with bright eyes. 'That's fine.'

Lizzie, smiling back, wondered how she could ever have thought him somehow below her because of his past. He was a dear, kind man, as Jane had tried to tell her. As Zek had tried to tell her.

'I think I shall go to Sydney Town,' she said at last, into the companionable quiet. 'If you will give me Mr Wilson's address, at least I shall have one acquaintance there, and perhaps he can find me work. No, my mind is made up. I know I will manage, and I have to stand on my own two feet. I must, for the child's sake.'

Their arguments had no effect, and in the end Lizzie just laughed at them and they gave up. When

Johnny had gone off, yawning, to bed, and the two women were left together, they spoke of the past. Old stories, old jokes, old tears. Jane found some plum cake, and reminding Lizzie it would soon be Christmas, handed her a piece.

'You've changed Liz,' she said softly. 'You've grown gentler somehow. You always seemed so . . . bandaged up, if you know what I mean. As if you was afraid to be yourself. Now you're not, and you're softer. Even your clothes are different, and the way your hair is . . . oh, you know! I never was good with words, like you.'

Lizzie laughed. 'You're certainly less volatile than you were, sister-mine!'

Jane scowled. 'If I knew what that meant I'd have something to say to you.'

Lizzie started to laugh.

'Liz . . . Liz, you can't really mean to go to Sydneyton. It's such a big place and . . . oh Lizzie . . .'

But Lizzie's jaw was firmly set. 'I mean it, love. I have to stand on my own two feet. I must! I can never go back to Zek. You have to see that. I never can. Now no more talk of it. I'll stay a while, I promise, but in the end I'll be off and you mustn't pretend to yourself that I won't.'

Jane sighed and bowed her head, but there was defeat in the droop of shoulder and mouth. Lizzie sighed, too, and for a moment fear of the future and grief of the past clouded her determination, but it was only for a moment. She pushed both aside firmly and lifting her own head looked with clear sight to the future.

CHAPTER
ELEVEN

THE day was clear and cloudless. A perfect January morning. Liz lifted her face to the blue heavens and smiled, ignoring the bump and rattle of the cart and the bustle of life about her. George Street was alive with the populace of Sydney Town, all eager to be about their business this fine summer's day. Lizzie felt the eagerness in the air, felt it stirring her own blood and spirit.

The time with Jane and Johnny had helped to rebuild her strength and courage. The terrible sickness had passed, though she still felt a trifle delicate at times. A visit to the new doctor in Evanstown, who had lately made his home there after arriving from London, confirmed Jane's diagnosis. Not that Lizzie had been worried it might be a mistake. The signs were much too clear.

Jane and Johnny . . . Lizzie smiled at the memory of them, and the happiness of the Christmas spent in their company. It had saddened her to have to go, but she knew that she must make a move. If she put it off for too long, she would have remained there in the circle of their love and protection indefinitely. And that was no good for Lizzie. She needed to stand on her own two feet.

Of Zek there had been no sign and no word. Not that she had expected to hear from him, Lizzie told herself sternly. He must be far too grateful to be rid of her honourably to pursue her.

Well, that was behind her. She had set her face to a new and bright future, and she would never turn around again.

So Lizzie told herself, as the cart set her down in Elizabeth Street, and she made her way, with her only luggage, the old and battered carry-bag, to a respectable boarding-house Johnny had given her the direction of. The woman who ran it was blowzy but kindly, and mothered her as Lizzie told her a little of her past. Her room was up a steep flight of stairs, and the woman panted and puffed up in front of her, gasping out meal times and rules and regulations in a hoarse voice.

'No men in the rooms, love, I don't have that sort here. And no takin' in washin' either. Meals downstairs, three times a day, and I feed my guests well if I do say so meself. You'll be comfortable, love?'

This last, was as Lizzie finally reached the doorway behind her and followed her in. The room was small, but tidy and comfortable. It would suit her well enough until she found work.

'Thank you, I will indeed,' Lizzie said, turning with a smile.

The big woman nodded—narrowed, curious eyes in a round, puffy face. Broken veins on her nose spoke of imbibing, secret or otherwise. Sometimes Lizzie thought the colony thrived not on sheep, wheat and convicts, but on rum.

'Where did you say you last worked?'

'Near Bathurst. I'm hoping to find more here.'

'Work!' The woman looked pitying, and a little scornful for such naivety. 'Little enough o' that here at the moment. Maybe you should have stayed in Bathurst. What was it you did there?'

Lizzie turned to the window. It was small paned,

and the glass a little warped, but it gave a view into the street and she looked with interest on to the traffic of Sydney Town.

'I was a housekeeper,' she said quietly.

The woman behind her shrugged, and turned away to the door, pausing on the landing. 'I wish you luck, love,' she said, more gently, 'but you'll be needin' it.'

Lizzie sighed at the sound of the closing door. The same story. It seemed so long ago that she and Jane had stood outside the laundry and faced the same predicament. But then luck had found them in the shape of Johnny. Luck would come again, it must. It was something she deserved after all her unhappiness.

Unhappiness? Her hand strayed to her belly and she smiled, thinking of the life that was growing there. Things were not so bad. She could never truly lose Zek, could she, when she was to bear his child?

She slept well and deeply, and rose hungry for the lavish breakfast. The other occupants of the establishment seemed unfriendly, or perhaps it was caution which prevented them from welcoming her. Besides, Lizzie did not wish to sit chattering to strangers. She had plans of her own, and lost no time in setting out into the thriving heart of Sydney Town.

She asked in shops at first, and then at a few of the grander houses, hoping for work as a servant or assistant, or word of where she might find it. She visited some agencies, but they seemed unhopeful in the extreme, and by the end of the day she felt a niggling worm of despair. But there was still Jason Wilson.

Lizzie had hoped she would not have to play upon his friendship, her pride rebelled a little at such a trick. But if she were desperate . . . And there was Zek's child to think of. With a sigh, she climbed the stairs to her little room. Tomorrow she would find Jason. There was no longer any room for pride.

Mr Jason Wilson lived on Hyde Park, and she had no trouble finding the house, a tall, redbrick place with great bay windows and a smooth, green lawn. She hesitated at the gate, wondering if she was doing the best thing, but the determination and desperation which had carried her thus far carried her on.

'Yes?'

The maid at the door eyed her insolently, but Lizzie was used by now to the attitude of the ex-felon, and merely demanded to see the master in a voice which sounded confident of success.

Jason Wilson was still breakfasting, and took some time to appear. But when he did his pleasure more than made up for Lizzie's wait in a dim little sitting-room which was the convict maid's revenge.

'Miss Banister! Oh Miss Banister, how marvellous.' The smile with which he greeted her dimmed a little at the edges, and he cocked his head to one side. 'Or should I say Mrs Gray?'

Her own smile trembled, but she lifted her head in the old way he remembered and said, 'Miss Banister will do very well, Mr Wilson.'

He came forward then to take her hands. 'I did not hope, when I gave my direction to your sister, that it would be you who took advantage of it!'

'I hope I am not taking advantage, sir, but I have need of your help.'

'Why Miss Banister—'

'Mr Wilson, I am looking for work, respectable work. I need to work—'

He was frowning a little, but did not seem as surprised by her request as she had expected. After a moment, he asked her to sit down, apologising for forgetting his manners, and she sat on a straight-backed, padded chair, grateful for its support.

'Miss Banister, when I heard of your marriage to Zek I was . . . I was rather sorry. Oh, forgive me if I pain you but I had thought you a woman of more foresight, and more sense. I thought you would recognise such a man for what he was!'

'Mr Wilson,' Lizzie said sharply and firmly, 'I do not wish to hear any more of what you have to say about my husband. The fact that he was not the man for me is neither here nor there. Now, if you will be good enough to tell me where I might ask for work, I shall trouble you no more.' She stared at him haughtily a moment before realising how wrongly she was going about things. Lizzie bit her lip. 'Oh sir, I'm that sorry! I never meant . . . I . . . oh dear.'

But he was laughing. 'Miss Banister, you are just as I remembered you. I'm so glad. I thought for a moment Zek had . . . well, no more of that,' with an uneasy eye on her. 'Of course I shall find you work. I shall do better than that! I am in the market for a housekeeper myself. My last one was good enough to hand in her papers last month when I demanded to know what had become of my best sherry. The fact that I objected to her selling it to her soldier friends was insulting to her, and she left for greener fields. I have not thought about replacing her, until now . . .'

Lizzie could hardly believe her ears, and took a moment to answer.

'I don't know what to say. You are so kind. I
don't want to trespass upon your kindness. If you
truly wish me to act as your housekeeper, I would
be more than pleased to repay your friendship with
hard work.'

'Truly, it is no favour I am doing you, Miss
Banister. I am more than glad to see you again, and
go on seeing you.'

Lizzie smiled, looking down at her hands. They
were rough from the work at The Thirsty Felon.
They had been softer not long ago, when Zek had
treated her like a pampered lady. But that was in
the past, and must remain so.

'I will get the girl to show you the housekeeper's
quarters, Miss Banister, and then you shall have tea
with me. If . . . that is, if you are still agreeable to
the idea.'

Lizzie sighed. 'Mr Wilson, I think I should tell
you something before I agree to any of your kind-
nesses.' And taking a deep breath she told him
about the baby.

'Miss Banister,' he said, a whisper. 'But Lord,
girl, you cannot call yourself "Miss" with such an
event on the way!'

Lizzie bit her lip. 'I had not thought of that. Oh
dear. I suppose I must be *Mrs* Banister.'

'Lizzie, does Zek know about this? He cannot
know, I am sure of it. Perhaps you should write him
and tell him I am looking after you?'

'No.' She stood up. 'If you do not wish me
to stay, then I will leave. I know it is a lot to ask,
but—'

Jason looked at her a long moment, remembering.

Remembering Zek his friend, and Zek so confident and sure of himself, so bitingly sarcastic of

Jason's proprieties and homilies, and his mockery of Jason's own spotless way of life. The thought of Zek's wife playing housekeeper to him, serving him, was a tremendous boost to his ego. It was a pity that she would not write to Zek, and he would never know. And never know about the child. For a moment he gazed into the future and saw himself playing the bountiful master, presenting gifts with an offhand manner while Lizzie wiped away grateful tears and gazed at him with the pathetic adoration of a whipped cur. That Lizzie would never look at anyone like that did not enter into his thoughts, and he smiled at the picture he had created for his own vanity.

'Mr Wilson?'

Jason puffed himself out, smiling suddenly with real pleasure. 'Miss Banister . . . *Mrs* Banister, I wish you to become my housekeeper above all things. Please stay.'

His smile was appealing. Lizzie hovered, wondering whether after all she was doing the right thing. But there was really no choice. In the end, she had already made her choice. She sighed and nodded.

'I hope I shall suit you, Mr Wilson. I shall certainly do my best to make your home a comfortable, well-run one. And of course, if yòu should wish to terminate my employ when the child . . .'

'Nonsense. I am your friend, Lizzie, as well as your employer. You must know that.'

'Thank you.'

He merely nodded, his smile hidden. He wondered briefly how it had come about that Zek and Lizzie had married; they had seemed so at odds aboard ship. Worlds apart in all things. It was strange to him that two such people could have come together even long enough to conceive a child . . .

'Mr Wilson? I said I shall have to collect my things from the boarding-house.'

'But of course. I will send someone around at once. No, I insist. I will call the girl now to show you your rooms.'

'Mr Wilson, you're far too kind. I only hope—'

But he held up his hand and would hear no more, and Lizzie was secretly grateful to have so many fears and worries taken out of her hands.

Thus began another part of her already eventful life. She worked hard, and it was far easier than it had been at Gray's. Sydney Town was enough like London to make it seem almost like coming home, and the house was so grand it was a pleasure to be in charge of its smooth running. Her wage was generous, too, but Jason Wilson didn't make the mistake of being over-generous and driving her away. He was a perfect employer, so kind, always complimenting her and praising her. The other servants watched them slyly, but Lizzie didn't care what went on in their petty minds. Gossip meant nothing to her now. She was too caught up in the growth of the child within her.

She had had to buy clothes to fit, and had purchased a number of tiny things to suit a girl or boy. But she already thought of it as a boy. A boy with Zek's eyes and Zek's wicked smile. Oh God, it still pained her like a dagger-thrust to think of him. Sometimes she woke in the night, her cheeks wet with tears, after dreaming of him. Once, she dreamed he had come to fetch her home and it seemed so real she was unprepared to face the reality of her situation.

Her white face stared back at her from the mirror

above the dresser. 'You are a fool, Lizzie Banister,' she whispered quietly, before her throat closed on shaking, wracking sobs.

If only he *would* come and fetch her . . . And where would that leave both of them? Miserable, of course. Him pining for his Angelica, and she loving him so much it was an agony and not being able to show it. If he fetched her she knew in her heart she would never be able to leave him again, never be able to summon up the strength of purpose. These months without him had been too hard for her to have to face them afresh.

And so she knew she must never, never see him again.

Jane wrote often, talking about the inn and how well it was going, and how clever Johnny was. She never mentioned Zek Gray, so Lizzie could only suppose he never came to inquire, and be grateful.

In June, by chance, she saw the obituary notice in the paper for Mr Thomas Bailey. It also mentioned his 'grieving wife Angelica'. The words swam before Lizzie's eyes, and she blinked to clear her head. She felt nausea in her stomach, churning, thinking of Angelica 'grieving'. Poor man. He was better dead.

They were both free now, Angelica and Zek. It was to be as it always should have been. They could be happy. She folded the paper with careful creases, trying to drum up something of gladness for Zek's future happiness. But she felt so numb it was difficult to be glad.

'Lizzie, you seem so pale,' Jason said, meeting her in the hall. 'Have you been overdoing it again. My dear girl, you know I neither want nor expect you to push yourself so hard at this stage of the game.'

She turned away to rearrange some flowers.

'Not at all!'

'Well, I sincerely hope not! I think I shall take you for a drive in the park today. It's not too cold, and if you rug up the sun will put a little colour into your cheeks. No, I insist!'

Lizzie forced her pale lips into a smile. It did no good to argue with him, when he was determined on treating her to some pleasure. But for a moment he had sounded so like Zek she felt sick with guilt and longing.

'Very well, Jason. But you're too good to me. You know you are. Housekeepers are not so . . . so coddled.'

His own smile was a little smug, but she hardly noticed as she turned away to fetch her cloak and bonnet. She moved slowly, but still gracefully enough, he thought. The child had not made her gross as some women, weighted down with their burden. He had had to put his foot down to prevent her wearing herself out with work, now that her time was near. She had been a little tearful, and he had comforted her with his arms, rocking her like a child herself. The memory was sweet. Zek's wife in his arms! Who would have thought it? It was only a pity Zek could never know of it.

It was a lovely day, and the winter offered them the warmth of her distant sun as they bowled along the cobbled streets. Jason smiled at her, complimenting her on the sparkle in her eyes. Lizzie returned the smile, though privately she thought the 'sparkle' more a glitter of fever. She was feeling distinctly unwell, and had been ever since she saw the paper, but was far too kind-hearted to say so.

Children and their nurses strolled, maid-servants giggled together, and were ogled by red-coated

soldiers. They passed the Hyde Park barracks, and
Lizzie watched the soldiers drilling, while Jason
told her how scandalous they were, his thin lips
curling in distaste. They were sentiments she would
once have joined in heartily, but now she couldn't
help but compare his telling with what Zek's would
have been.

Some thin-legged children were playing with a
scrawny dog on the side of the road, as they
rounded the corner.

'Lizzie, what is it? Something is troubling you.'

After a moment she said, 'I saw the paper this
morning, Jason.'

He said nothing, and she glanced at him wondering if she need say more. But he seemed to know
what she meant, and she thought with a sense of
unease that the look on his face was almost satisfied. Like a cat which has laid the bait of a trap
and seen the mouse caught and crushed. The
thought was so totally foreign in connection with
him, and so unpleasant, she thrust it away.

It was at that moment that the dog ran across the
road in front of them, and one of the ragged boys
followed.

Lizzie screamed, snatching at the reins. Jason
turned, jerking the horse's head around. The animal, thoroughly frightened, rose up on its hind
legs, rocking the occupants of the gig about like
toys. Lizzie screamed again, clutching the sides and
trying not to be thrown out on to the road. Jason
struggled, face red, to bring the animal under control. He did so, eventually, and wiping his brow
with a gloved hand, turned with concern to Lizzie.

'Mrs Banister . . . Lizzie, are you all right?'

The conversation of moments before was forgotten. She lifted her head, her face ghastly white, and

tried to smile. 'I think . . . I think you had best get me home, Jason my dear.'

'You are hurt!'

'No, no, it is not that. The baby, Jason, has chosen this moment, of all moments, to decide to be born.'

Somehow they got back to the house, and Jason sent for the doctor.

Lizzie was taken upstairs to her room, and one of the maids helped her into bed, undressing her and settling her more comfortably. The pain was sharp and frequent, and she knew with a sense of helpless fear that there was not long to go. The maid seemed helpless and inexperienced too, and after offering her a glass of water and plumping her pillows for the tenth time, stood by wringing her hands and wishing for the doctor to hurry.

He arrived at last, and shooed the woman out to fetch hot water and towels. He was a big man, with big hands, and Lizzie shrank from him.

'Here now!' he boomed, 'behave yourself, girl. I'm not going to hurt you any more than I have to. Let's see this babe who's in such a hurry to get on with living, shall we?'

Lizzie bit her lips as he examined her, humming all the while as if he were teeing up for a game of golf.

'Aye, I see how it is. Impatient little blighter, ain't he?'

'He?' Lizzie whispered.

'Or she?' he eyed her a moment, then smiled. 'Cheer up, my girl. It'll be all over before you know it, and you'll be as right as rain again.'

It wasn't over before she knew it, but the baby was in a hurry to be born. Lizzie did as the doctor told her, trying not to scream when the pain grew too great. When at last, with a great push of her body, she thrust Zek's child out into the world, the relief was so great she fell into a swoon. She came around moments later to the glow of lamps in the dim room and the doctor's voice, hearty as ever, booming:

'I said a "he", didn't I?'

Her eyes focused on the white-wrapped bundle, and with trembling arms she took it from him. A red, angry face, a mass of dark hair and tiny, tiny fists. Oh God, so tiny. She felt the warmth of tears on her cheeks and looked up at the man with humility.

'Oh,' she whispered, 'thank you.'

He let out a great guffaw of laughter. 'You had a mite to do with it too, my girl! Never seen such an impatient, fighting babe. Your man must be a fighter, too, eh?'

'Yes,' she whispered, and looked again into the pinched little face.

A boy for Zek. She had no hesitation in the naming of him. Only one name would ever do. When she looked up again the doctor had gone and the maid was hovering about, ready to remove the child to the makeshift cot. Lizzie let him go reluctantly, already feeling the first threads of exhaustion winding insidiously about her limbs and thoughts, drawing her into sleep.

CHAPTER
TWELVE

'Lizzie! Should you be up so soon?'

Jason started to his feet in dismay, as Lizzie appeared in the doorway of the breakfast-room.

She laughed almost like her old self. 'I've been resting for a week now! Please, Jason, don't condemn me to any more of it. I'll go mad.'

He smiled, but still looked worried as he came to take her hands. He noted then the lines of strain at her eyes, and the new slimness of her body. He had been so used to seeing her big with the child he had forgotten how slender she was. But for all that, she looked well and healthy.

'Lizzie, are you sure—'

'Oh nonsense! I'm perfectly well. I'm only worried you'll be handing me my notice, I've neglected you so, Jason.'

'I would never do that,' he said quietly.

She looked at him then with a start. He was looking down at her, his rather cool blue eyes warm and . . . yes, and loving. Lizzie felt a shock of surprise and dismay. He must not love her, he must not. She had nothing to give in return. All her love was centred on the tiny scrap of humanity upstairs in his cot, and Zek . . . but Zek was gone.

But Jason had turned away, offering her a chair. 'Now that you're here you may as well breakfast with me. Please,' when she hesitated. 'I've missed you, Lizzie. I didn't realise how much I depended upon your company until these past few days.'

Lizzie sat down, pouring herself some coffee and buttering a slice of toast. She really was ravenous now that she had regained her figure.

She dared a glance at Jason under her lashes. He was staring down the table at her, and smiled back.

'Lizzie, you have a fine son. I took the liberty of peeping in on him yesterday. He is your image. What will you call him?'

Her lashes swept down and up again. 'I'll call him after his father, Jason. I think he is very much his father's son.'

Jason looked disconcerted, but hid it by attacking his eggs and bacon. In fact, he was angry. Zek should have been forgotten long ago. What was he, in comparison to Jason himself? Nothing. A swaggering, bragging, bullying ladies' man, who cared for no one but himself and his own bodily pleasures. What had he done for Lizzie? Compared to Jason he had done nothing. And now Lizzie, who owed him so much and who should by now have been kissing his boots for a little affectionate attention, was planning to hold Zek Gray up to her son like a . . . a guiding light!

Jason had pictured the boy, yesterday, when he was older, running to him for guidance, running to him, calling him 'Father', and Lizzie blushingly correcting him but, glancing to Jason, smiling and hoping that one day . . . He had even decided she should call the boy 'Jason', in gratitude for all he had done in the sheltering of her. Of course, he thought, chewing on a piece of bacon, he would never marry her. How could he? Even if she were to divorce Zek she would be beneath him. A divorced woman was a scandalous thing in the circles

Jason moved in. Perhaps, one day, he would take her as his mistress. But his wife? Never.

Lizzie, knowing nothing of these thoughts, rose to her feet with a smile.

'Now, I really must get back to work, Jason. I promise you a delicious dinner tonight, just to make up for my laziness.'

'I won't be in,' he said coldly.

Her face fell. She looked so crestfallen and so adorable he almost relented. But the memory of Zek held him silent. She would just have to learn who was her true benefactor!

Lizzie sighed. Poor Jason. She had hurt him. Well, she would just have to make it up to him by extra hard work and tender care of his comfort. With a nod of her head, she set about putting the house, and the servants, to rights.

Jason was true to his word, and stayed out that evening, but he was in the following one and Lizzie made a fuss of him, smiling and treating him so like a king he was flattered and pleased, and eyed her under his lashes over the array of dishes. She looked beautiful tonight, aglow and shining with what could only be happiness. Dark hair caught back from her face and neck, her throat and shoulders exposed by the low neckline of the gown. Long, slim fingers beckoned and dismissed servants with assurance. She had become very assured since the birth of little Zek. She had matured into a striking woman.

Jason Wilson felt a stirring in his loins. By God, why should he wait to have her as his mistress? She was under his roof and available. She would come to him from gratitude if not love, if he played his cards right. He smiled at the thought of her lying against his pillows, surrendering herself to him with a gentle smile. Or perhaps she would be like a wildcat, fighting the urges of her own body as well as his, until he subdued her. Broke her to his hand.

'Jason?'

He started at the sound of her voice, and she smiled.

'I was miles away, Lizzie. I'm sorry. What did you say?'

By the gentleness of his voice she knew she was totally forgiven for the pain she had caused him and her smile broadened. 'I merely asked if you wished more meat, Jason.'

He shook his head. 'Thank you, but no. I am more than sated.'

Or would be, soon enough. The thought shook him to the roots of his proper, puritanical being. It was a dark thought, a wicked thought, and yet strangely exciting. He wanted her, and by God he would have her whatever anyone said. He deserved her, after all he had done for her, and all the inconvenience he had been put to over her. Besides, if he was to vanquish Zek for ever he must possess her totally, as Zek had done. Only then would Zek be truly dead for her.

'Lizzie,' he said quietly, 'I wish to speak to you about something . . . something rather important. Can you come into the study?'

His voice, serious and yet oddly stilted, brought her head up. Her eyes met his, questioning, but she smiled and nodded. 'Of course. I shall ask for coffee to be served in there. Or would you prefer tea?'

'Coffee, I think. And port. You will have port with me, Lizzie?'

He poured two glasses, and sank down in one of the chairs by the warmth of the fire, while Lizzie

occupied the other. She tried to sit still, gazing into
the flames, while her mind was racing to be back
upstairs with her son. He would be hungry. And yet
Jason was her employer, more than that, her
friend, and could not be denied. He had been so
good to her, so very good . . .

He was speaking. She listened idly, still turning
the glass in her fingers. For a moment she didn't
understand what he was saying, or perhaps it was
just that she couldn't quite believe the evidence of
her own senses.

He was saying he cared for her, but couldn't
marry her. He was saying he wished her to be his
mistress. He was saying how much he craved her.
He was saying so much she shook her head, lifting
one shaking hand to her brow.

'Jason! I hardly know . . . Jason!'

He frowned into her eyes. She looked shocked,
and her fingers shook on the glass, shaking the wine
on to her skirts. He took the glass from her, clasping her wrist and pulling her to her feet.

'Lizzie,' he murmured into her hair, letting the
scent of her intoxicate him. It was all he could do
not to push her down on to the brocade-covered
sofa and take her there and then. But he must bide
his time, he knew that much. If she came willingly,
the victory over Zek would be all the sweeter.

She seemed content to rest against him, as he
stroked her back and let his lips rest on her temple.

'Jason, I don't know what to say. You've been so
good to me . . .'

Then isn't it time you thought about paying, he
thought viciously, but did not speak it aloud.

'I like you. I do. But I do not love you.'

As if love had aught to do with it, Jason thought.
'But I need you, Lizzie,' he wheedled. 'I am beg-

ging you. You say I have been good to you. Can you not be good to me, just a little?'

She sighed, and drew away. 'I will have to think upon it, Jason. You will forgive me if I have time to think?'

Her dark eyes searched his desperately, and he nodded. 'Of course,' he said, but in a disappointed way.

After a moment she kissed his cheek, and with a swish of skirts, hurried from the room.

Jason Wilson drank from his glass and smiled into the flames. She would fall into his hand like a ripe plum, he thought with satisfaction. Zek's wife, in his hand. It would be all right after all then. It was going to turn out very nicely indeed.

Upstairs, Lizzie held her little son in her arms and humming, rocked him against her. He was so tiny, so helpless, so dependent upon her. And she was so dependent upon Jason Wilson. She had not realised how much until now. And how much she owed him. Oh yes, she could run away back to Johnny and Jane, but . . . but she owed him something, and if this was to be her payment, then should she not give it with good grace?

Her face flamed at the thought of Jason and she . . . And she felt a curl of nausea in her stomach. Zek had been her lover and her love. Could she ever give herself to another? Could she betray Zek, even while he betrayed her?

The problem was beyond her, and she dropped her chin to rest on the dark head of little Zek. She had him to think about, after all. Her baby, her son. Perhaps she was being selfish in thinking about her own feelings. She should think of little Zek. She might even grow content with being Jason's . . . Jason's . . .

'Oh Lord,' she groaned, 'I cannot. I just cannot!'

Jason didn't speak of it the following morning, for which she was grateful, but she knew he was awaiting her decision, and he could hardly be expected to wait forever. In the afternoon, she set out for the markets, her basket over her arm, her bonnet tied firmly under her chin.

Jason watched her go from the study window, a look of smug satisfaction curving his features. She was struggling, but they were weak struggles, and soon he would pull her in. He thought he had played her very nicely last night, and he had been content to stay quiet today and let her weaken herself with her own arguments. But she would give in in the end. She had no choice.

Lizzie, knowing nothing of his gaze or his thoughts, strode away briskly, enjoying the fresh breeze, the chill sting on her cheeks making her feel intensely alive.

She had put aside all thoughts of Jason today, and thought instead of her son. She smiled, pausing in crossing the road to bring his face to mind. He was already far too handsome for his own good, so like Zek . . .

The streets were busy, and Lizzie avoided a large woman with a child in each hand. She smiled at a man who tipped his hat at her with a warm smile. She felt pretty today. Pretty and accomplished and needed. Had Jason given that feeling to her, with his propositions of last night? Or was it just that she was getting over Zek, at last?

Zek. No, she would never get over Zek. Even the thought of him now, in this bustling street, brought tears stinging to her eyes. She stopped, resting against the wall of a bank, and blinked.

And blinked again, wondering for a horrified

moment if she had conjured up his image like some magician, some Merlin. For there he stood, by the kerb, his back to her, talking to a woman in a green pelisse. At least, from the back, it looked very like him. Broad shoulders, trim hips, dark hair curling at his collar. She trembled, resting heavily against the cold stones, telling herself she must, she *must* be mistaken.

And then he turned, and she knew she wasn't.

It was Zek. Zek, a little thinner perhaps, and a little paler, but it was Zek all the same. And as she stared in wonder and disbelief his eyes fixed on her. They widened, as though he thought he had seen a spirit, and then he was striding forward, making for her as though they were alone in the world, and not in the middle of a thronging crowd. And the look on his face made her afraid.

The blood rushed under her skin, and at the same time the strength poured back into her body. She turned and began to run, her basket jolting against her side. Her feet gained speed, and she hoisted up the bulk of her skirts, brushing by pedestrians without care or thought apart from escape.

Zek! He had come to destroy himself, and her. She must not let him catch her, she must not! If he did, if he took her back . . . Lord, it did not bear thinking about. Her bonnet slid back, and her hair fell untidily down her back, long and curling and uncontrollable.

'Lizzie!' he called, but his voice was faint, and daring a glance over her shoulder, she saw him back at the last corner. He was stuck behind a couple of men moving a large sideboard across the footpath from a parked dray to the doorway of a shop. Even as she looked, she saw him thrust one of them aside and hurry on.

Lizzie, in desperation, turned up a narrow side-
street and into the dark, open door of a little shop.
A dim, musty interior, row upon row of bottles and
potions. She stood panting, her head spinning. It
was an apothecary's shop. The smell of spices and
exotic medicines was overpowering; she could hear
the proprietor discussing the benefits of one of his
mixtures to a large lady with a tartan shawl about
her massive shoulders.

Lizzie darted a swift, frightened glance over her
own shoulder to the doorway, and slid behind a row
of shelving, gripping her hands so tightly the blood
came under the bite of her nails.

She stood there for some minutes, pretending a
fascination for the bottles' contents she could never
otherwise have felt. The large lady left satisfied, a
packet tucked under her arm, and the proprietor, a
little man with clothing that smelt of camphor,
came to hover about Lizzie, pointing out various
products and extolling their virtues.

Zek did not appear. The square of light that was
the doorway remained empty. When she could
pretend interest no longer, Lizzie smiled at the
man, and stepped cautiously out into the street.

The narrow thoroughfare was deserted of anyone remotely resembling Zek. One end of the lane
was blocked off by a wrought-iron gate that looked
far too high to clamber over and far too narrow for
her to squeeze through. Lizzie sighed, and turned
back towards the street she had so lately left. She
walked slowly and carefully towards the corner,
blinking in the glare after the dark little shop. Her
bonnet was still resting down her back, and she
made some repairs to it and her hair, while she tried
to whip up enough courage to step out into the
passing crowd.

It was so easy, she thought. She would tag on to a group and soon be far away, out of reach, safe. Lizzie took a breath and stepped out into the street.

He was standing some three yards from her, and saw her at once. Somehow she had known that he would be. She had known, all the time she was planning her escape, that there would be no chance of it. So when he began to walk towards her she did not even try to run away, but stood like one facing a firing squad.

He seemed taller than she remembered, and she looked up into the dark, bleak eyes as though it were yesterday she had seen them last.

After a moment he said in a voice as bleak as his eyes, 'Am I to assume you do not wish even to speak with me, Lizzie?'

From somewhere her voice replied, 'You can assume what you will.'

'Lizzie—'

'We have nothing to say, Zek. Nothing.' Her voice cracked with the strain of keeping it steady and cool.

'Lizzie, did you mean what you said in that letter you left me in Bathurst?'

Lizzie remembered the harsh black writing on the sterile white paper. 'Of course,' she said, and lifted her chin at him proudly, while inside her heart was tearing in two and her teeth were clenched to stop the sobs.

His eyes slid over her face, her untidy hair, her new gown. 'You look beautiful,' he said then, and smiled.

It was a parody of his old smiles, and made her sad. Was life not good to him then? Was Angelica not as loving as he wished?

'You're too kind.'

His lashes swept down to hide his eyes, and he said, 'May I ask where you are staying?'

'I'm working. As a housekeeper.'

He smiled again, something of humour in his eyes and mouth. She was eaten up with love for him. Every line of his face, every muscle, every inch of him. She wanted to put her arms about him and hold him to her and never let him go. And she knew, sickeningly, that she could not, could never do so. He belonged to someone else and always had. She had been his wife briefly, for her, the best part of her life. But that was over.

'How is the farm?' she managed.

'Well enough, in material terms,' he said.

'How is . . . is everyone?'

'Everyone is well. And you, Lizzie? Are you well?'

'Perfectly.'

They were like strangers. She watched his dark brows come down, his darker eyes subjecting her to a piercing, thorough search of her face and figure.

'You do look blooming,' he said at last, and there was a wealth of suspicion in his voice.

'Why shouldn't I be? I'm happy,' she said.

'Obviously,' he said, with distaste, and looked away as though dismissing her.

After a moment she found the strength to say, 'I must get on. I'm glad I saw you again, Zek. I hope you're happy.'

'Lizzie . . .'

'I really must go. I'm sorry, Zek.'

'Do you want a divorce, Lizzie?'

She was shocked. She turned, her still-puritan brain reeling. A divorce! Of all things abhorrent to Cook. Divorce! No one of any breeding, any proper standards divorced. Hadn't Jason said himself last night that he would never expect her to divorce Zek? And yet, was it not an obvious ending to their marriage? Had she really imagined Zek would be content to leave things as they were? If he loved Angelica and wanted to marry her, then he must divorce Lizzie. She licked her lips, her voice a squeak of horror and despair:

'Oh I . . . Zek, I can't. It's so . . . so final . . .'

What had Cook said? 'Loose women and Americans divorce their husbands. Ladies do not.'

A flicker showed in his dark eyes. 'Can you not, Lizzie?' A smile. 'I thought to be final was what you wanted?'

'But . . . it's degrading, Zek. There would be a scandal.'

'You have a choice then, Lizzie. You will divorce me, or return to live with me as a proper wife. I will not allow half-measures.'

She licked her lips again, like a trapped animal. She had been in charge of the situation only seconds ago, and now somehow he had taken over.

'Couldn't we just go on as we have?' she whispered, her face growing alarmingly pale.

Jason would never let her stay if there was a scandal. She would be thrown out, with little Zek. Everything would be ruined and . . . Oh Lord, how *could* she go home with him after all that had happened?

Zek was shaking his head slowly and finally. 'Divorce it must be, Lizzie. We shall have to go through the courts. God knows how long it will take, but it must be done. I suppose I must be the one to make the sacrifice, and find proof of my adultery? I shall have to rake up some harlot from the Rocks to plead with me. Or would you prefer to . . . but no perhaps not,' as her eyes flashed fire.

'Then I shall set about it at once. The newspapers, I suppose, will have a field day. They love a nice meaty scandal.'

Lizzie knew that only too well. She remembered one case just lately, splashed in heavy print across front pages, the prose flowery, insidious, cruel. Language she herself had read guiltily but avidly, disbelievingly, and yet . . . yes, half-convinced all the while it must be partly true. 'No smoke without fire', as the old saying went.

Zek had taken her arm firmly in his. 'Give me your direction,' he said quietly, 'and I will drive back with you. We have much to discuss, Lizzie.'

She had walked several paces before she remembered she must not let him worm his way into her life again. For his own sake. And yet, was the divorce not for his own sake? Hesitantly, she allowed him to lead her on in the direction of some cabs.

'I will give you your divorce,' she said in a brittle, cold voice. 'There is no need to come back with me. I will write to you.'

'Oh, but there is. And the fact that you so obviously don't want me to see where you live is very intriguing.'

'There is no point to it, Zek!' she cried in desperation.

His hand merely tightened, and he said cruelly, 'Stop snivelling and tell me where we're going.'

Confused, torn apart with longing and pain, Lizzie told him the address. She knew by the satisfied smile on his mouth that he had no idea whose it was. He was merely pleased at his own success. Why was he pleased? A divorce would be as unpleasant and painful for him and Angelica as it would be for her and little Zek.

'I read . . . I read in the paper,' she managed. 'About Mr Bailey. I was sorry.'

His eyes turned to her in the shadowy interior of the cab, distant and unreadable. 'So was I, Lizzie.'

Her mouth opened, and closed. She could not ask about that woman; she could not! It was asking too much of her.

'How did you get here, Lizzie?' he said quietly. 'You were gone when I got back that evening. How did you leave Bathurst?'

'I took a place on a wagon going to . . . to Sydney Town.'

'You must have been desperate.'

There seemed no answer to that, so she didn't attempt one, but turned to look out of the window. After a moment the cab came to a stop and she hurried to step down out of it on to the road. As she did so a carriage came past at speed, so close to her she felt the breeze of it on her cheek, and stumbled, falling back against Zek as he too descended. He caught her, his arms going about her hard.

For a moment she was pressed close to his chest, feeling his heart beat, the warmth of his body through his clothing. There was great strength in his arms, she had forgotten how much. She felt ill with longing, and pushed angrily away in case he should feel it.

His face was as pale as hers, and he seemed to be labouring under some great burden, so that he spun away to pay the driver almost clumsily. When he turned back again he was calm, and cold.

'Well, lead the way,' he said like a whiplash, and she went stumbling ahead.

'There is something I should tell you, before you go in,' she said, stumbling over her words as she did her steps.

'Such as what?' he retorted bitterly. 'If you want to tell me you hate my guts, I already know it.'

'Zek, no!'

'And if you want to tell me you're shacked up with some other man, I think I know that too, and I intend to break his back.'

He meant it. She saw the rage glittering in his eyes, and wondered why. He had tricked her, and now he meant to do violence to Jason. It made no sense!

'Please, it's not like that. I work for him. I would never . . .' But hadn't she been about to become Jason's mistress? And all for gratitude and fear?

But it was too late. Jason must have seen them arrive, and was in the hall. Zek's eyes widened in disbelief, and then disgust. He looked at Lizzie as though she were dirt, his mouth curling.

'So, that's the way it is,' he said gratingly. 'Very pretty.'

'Zek,' she whispered, and then, turning imploringly to Jason, 'He won't listen to me, Jason. Please, tell him I am only your housekeeper.'

But Jason had waited too long for this moment to do anything of the sort. He looked at her, and then at Zek, and he smiled. He saw in the other man's face more than Lizzie could see, in her own grief and pain. He saw the agony of a love lost, and the biting jealousy of his woman living with another man, and knew with a sting of malignant pleasure that he could vanquish and destroy Zek Gray forever.

'Why deny it,' he said softly, and watched Lizzie's mouth fall open in disbelief.

Zek started forward, fists clenching, but Jason stepped back saying quickly, 'Why not lose gracefully, man! Admit you've lost. Lizzie is mine and stays mine. Did you hear me? For once in your life admit your fatal charm has failed!'

The bitter hatred in his voice was so clear, Lizzie turned to him in amazement, remembering suddenly that other time, when he had let her see the newspaper. It was as if she were seeing him for the first time as he really was.

It was doubtful if Zek even heard him. He had started forward again, fists clenching, and grabbed Jason by his immaculate shirt front, lifting him a little from the floor despite his superior height, and his dark face was a mask of rage.

Lizzie flung herself at him, pulling at his arms. 'Don't! Zek, he's lying. Please, it's not true!'

Thank God, thank God, she thought, that it wasn't true. One more day, and she might never have been able to say that to him again.

'Lying is he!' Zek flung Jason from him.

The other man struck against a table, knocking it and its valuable cargo to the floor. He struggled to his feet, trying to straighten his clothing. A servant came running from the kitchens, but Jason waved him angrily away, his face flushed with anger, triumph and exertion.

Zek turned on Lizzie, his black eyes aglitter as they had been that night in their bedroom after she had flirted with Leigh. Lizzie watched him come, holding out her hands futilely.

'Zek, please . . .'

'Zek, please,' he whispered, vicious in his parody. 'What do you think I've been feeling all this time? Knowing you'd left me because you couldn't stand the sight of me? Knowing you hated my guts, and you were willing to brave God knew what to get away from me. But I let you go, because I thought that was what you wanted. I let you tear

me apart with worry and fear and . . . yes, and
grief. Because I thought that was what you wanted.
And when finally I could stand it no longer and
came after you, I find you in a little love-nest,
blooming. Bloody blooming with health!'

'You sound as if you're sorry I'm not dead!' she
shouted.

He stopped then, and she knew she had made a
bad mistake. After a moment he said, in a dead,
quiet voice:

'It was a trick. All a trick. You were never ill. It
was all a trick by you and your sister. I knew there
was something wrong. I knew it! I called on her and
she said you were in Sydney Town. She wouldn't
tell me where, but I found the boarding-house
where you stayed, before your luggage was col-
lected. In God's name, Lizzie, why did you trick
me?'

Lizzie felt the tears in her eyes, and whispered,
'She didn't mean to hurt anyone, and I *was* ill. Zek,
I was ill . . .'

'A trick,' he said, seemingly not hearing her soft
words. 'You are just like all the rest. All the
Angelicas of this world. I had thought you different, but you're just the same.'

Lizzie stared at him in amazement. He had
spoken as though he hated Angelica. And that was
impossible. Wasn't it? It turned everything topsy-
turvy. She didn't understand.

'But you love Angelica!' she cried. 'That was
why . . .'

Her voice halted him and he turned to look at her
narrowly. 'Love her? She's the biggest bitch out.
You know that. I never loved her. I love . . . *loved*
you. Lizzie, I loved you.'

It was said so quietly, she couldn't question its

truth. Her legs were like jelly. She sat down abruptly on the hall chair, staring up at him with huge dark eyes in a deathly white face. From behind them Jason said:

'Get out of here, Zek! You're not wanted. Lizzie belongs to me.'

They ignored him. He no longer existed for either of them.

Zek said, in a voice quiet and drained, and yet so sincere she could no longer doubt him, 'I'd known a lot of women. I'd thought myself in love more than once. I was a fool to think that, because when I did fall in love it hit me like a stone. I didn't know what to do about it, Lizzie. I didn't know whether to sweep her off her feet or play it safe, what to say . . . She was so different from all the rest, you see. Perhaps that was why I loved her. She had no poise, no simperings, no coy giggles. I'm talking about you, Lizzie. I think,' he went on softly, thoughtfully, as though speaking of something so long past it was now only a sweet memory, 'I think I must have loved you from the moment I kissed you, thinking you were Jane. Only you weren't, and from that moment on you kept showing me how different you were. God knows, you weren't my type at all; or so I thought in my conceit. But I fell like a ton of bricks for Lizzie Banister dressed in sackcloth, who let me feel the sharp edge of her tongue at every conceivable opportunity. And who nearly died, and who I determined then not to leave alone again—I would have come back even if your sister hadn't invited me. And on whom I squandered my money and wore out my heart, when she suddenly became ill as I'd been warned she would, and who I tried so desperately to make jealous on every occasion, and who never seemed to care less.'

His eyes were bleak and empty, and he went on in that terrible, stranger's voice, 'The thought of you dying was crucifying me, Lizzie, but I would never have left you to it. You should have known that. I would have stayed until the end; you were all that was precious to me. I wanted to treasure every moment left to us. I loved you that much. Which is why, when you wanted to go, I let you go. Until now.'

'Until now,' she whispered.

Jason, behind him, had straightened, and lifting the chair was coming up behind him. Lizzie with a screech flung herself at Jason, tearing at his face with her nails. He swore, struggling to throw her off, and then Zek pushed her aside and with a well-aimed blow sent him crashing to the ground.

There was a silence while Zek stood over the prone body, panting slightly, eager to continue if Jason had the strength to get up. When he didn't, he turned again to Lizzie, perhaps preparing himself for an onslaught from her.

But Lizzie, glaring down at Jason's face, said, 'Good! He was hateful. I thought he was my friend, but he was a hateful liar. He was eaten up with hatred for you, Zek. I can see that now. He only gave me work so that he could hold it over you, and . . .' But it hadn't come to the final victory, and she could only thank God.

Zek was gazing at her with suspicious, puzzled eyes.

'Lizzie?'

A maid clattered to the top of the staircase, her hands wringing, her eyes bulging at the scene below. 'Oh, Mrs Banister! The baby. All the noise has frightened him and . . . can you come. I just don't know what to do.'

'Oh no.'

Lizzie rushed up the stairs, hardly pausing to catch breath before heading into the bedroom. Little Zek was bawling his healthy lungs out. She lifted him up carefully, cradling him against her, and it was only when, crooning, she turned, and she realised Zek had followed her up. He looked like a man struck to stone, and she flushed under his incredulous, wondering gaze.

'And don't dare say he's anyone else's,' she snapped, 'because only your son would be such a . . . such a noisy, disruptive, bullying . . .'

'My God woman, you've got a lot to answer to!' he shouted, and when the child wailed at the unfamiliar sound, 'Why the hell didn't you tell me?'

'I didn't know myself, until Jane told me. I overheard you talking to Edna Tucker and I thought I was dying. Jane laughed her head off.'

His eyes were black and angry.

Little Zek sobbed, but softly now, and Lizzie cuddled him to her, her own voice softening. 'Oh Zek, I thought you loved Angelica. I thought I was a burden to you, when you wanted so to be with her. I kept remembering Thomas Bailey, and how he was . . . you know, clutching on to Angelica's skirts when she plainly wanted him dead and gone. I couldn't have borne that, Zek.'

'You thought what!' he ground out. 'After what I'd told you about it being over between her and me?'

'She was so beautiful, and clever, and . . . what man could resist her? And you seemed so unhappy . . . so troubled. I thought I was doing that to you. And then, when I saw you kissing her the night of the party . . . Zek, it was the bitter end for me!'

He spun away, to the window, and stood there

against the light, hands resting on the sill, knuckles clenched white as though he struggled with some great pressure within himself. Whatever it was he overcame it, for when Lizzie turned back from placing the now docile baby into its cot, he was watching her.

'I was Angelica's lover once,' he said at last. 'But I haven't been for a long time. She was too greedy and too selfish, Lizzie. After I met you, Angelica was not even in the running.'

It had been a dream until then. But now, looking into his face, the black eyes gleaming, she believed it. Handsome, cynical Zek Gray loved her. Loved Lizzie Banister; uncompromising, plain Lizzie Banister, who was so afraid of scandal she had lost her head and let him back into her life . . .

Or rather, he had loved her. Once. Her heart plummeted. His love had worn out; he was weary of her. It was all her own fault, too, so there was no use crying. But the tears had already started down her cheeks.

'Zek,' she whispered, and took a shaky step forward, 'I'm so sorry. I never knew. Oh Zek, I do love you so. Do you think you could forgive me?'

He caught her, pulling her against him and holding her so fast she could feel every muscle of his big body. 'Forgive you?' he muttered. 'When I was ready to tear Sydney Town apart to find you? I'll never forgive you.'

Crying and laughing, she said, 'Oh Zek, I've been so miserable. Every time I looked at little Zek I could only think of you.'

'Lizzie, Lizzie,' he breathed, kissing her face, as though he meant to mark every square inch of it before he found her lips. He pushed back her cloud of dark hair, his hand shaking. His eyes gleamed down at her. 'And you even intended to keep the knowledge of my son from me? Surely that was carrying self-sacrifice too far, my love?'

'I was afraid your honour would bring you back to me, even though your heart was Angelica's.'

'I was a fool ever to let you go; as big a fool as you were staying away from me, Lizzie. We have a lot to make up for, haven't we, Lizzie-mine?'

'Yes, Zek.'

'Tell me you love me.'

She met his black eyes, leaning back trustingly in his strong arms. He was altogether too sure of himself, was her handsome, wonderful husband. And it seemed a shame to spoil him further, by leaning closer and telling him in a whisper just how much she loved him.